# THE VOICE OF AN ANGEL

Among the U.S. Marines who fought against the Japanese in World War II was twenty-one-year-old Corporal William Devers, who considered himself an agnostic. No amount of arguing, Bible-quoting, or coercion by his fellow Marines or the chaplain could sway him. During the company's first major encounter with the Japanese, a number of the unit were killed and the chaplain was wounded. In great pain, the chaplain called to Devers, "My ... left pocket ... take it ... *please* ... Last night I had a dream. In the dream, an angel appeared and told me that I had to make you take the Bible. Take it son ... *please*." Devers shoved the Bible into his shirt pocket to satisfy the wounded man.

Twenty minutes later, Corporal Devers' squad stumbled right into a Japanese patrol, and before he knew what had happened he was on the ground, his mind fading into the darkness, certain he was dying. When he came to, he felt a ripple of pain shoot through his chest, but there was no blood. The bullet had torn into the Bible he carried in his pocket, ending its journey at the book of *Psalms* which read:

> *"A thousand shall fall at thy side,*
> *and ten thousand at thy right hand;*
> *but it shall not come nigh thee."*

# ANGELS BESIDE YOU

## JAMES PRUITT

AVON BOOKS ◆ NEW YORK

Unless otherwise indicated, all Scripture quotations are taken from the King James Version of the Bible. Those marked GNB are passages from the Good News Bible, copyright 1976 by the American Bible Society. Reprinted by permission. Grateful acknowledgment is made to the following for permission to reprint previously published material: Doubleday and Company: Excerpts from ''Heroes and Legends Of World War One'' by Arch Whitehouse. Copyright 1964. *Guidepost* Magazine: ''A Battle Poem.'' Copyright 1993 Guidepost Associates, Inc., Carmel, New York. Reprinted by permission.

ANGELS BESIDE YOU is an original publication of Avon Books. This work has never before appeared in book form.

AVON BOOKS
A division of
The Hearst Corporation
1350 Avenue of the Americas
New York, New York 10019

Copyright © 1994 by James Pruitt
Published by arrangement with the author
Library of Congress Catalog Card Number: 94-94342
ISBN: 0-380-77766-5

First Avon Books Printing: December 1994

AVON TRADEMARK REG. U.S. PAT. OFF. AND IN OTHER COUNTRIES, MARCA REGISTRADA, HECHO EN U.S.A.

Printed in the U.S.A.

RA   10  9  8  7  6  5  4  3  2  1

# Acknowledgments

This book could never have been written without the help of my good friend Tom Colgan. I owe him a debt of gratitude for his confidence in me. I would also like to thank the research departments of Oklahoma University and East Central University in Ada, Oklahoma, for their helpful suggestions and valuable background research that aided me in contacting the principal or relatives of those whose stories are told here.

I am eternally grateful to Dr. Billy Graham, who offered a wonderful letter of encouragement when informed of my task.

I especially want to thank the thousands of men and women of our armed forces, both past and present, who give of themselves unselfishly twenty-four hours a day so that we may enjoy the freedom and security of this great country—among them my son, Airman First Class Jason W. Pruitt.

I wish to thank my loving wife, Charlotte, and my daughter, Angela, for their encouragement and loving support, which sustained me through many long hours of research and late-night writing.

Finally, a thank-you to my guardian angel, who I am certain has been severely tested over the last forty-eight years, but still remains with me wherever I go . . .

# Contents

# CONTENTS

# Introduction

THE MOTIVATION FOR WRITING THIS BOOK CAME FROM two sources. One was a highly interesting special segment on angels that I happened to catch on an evening newsmagazine show. The story involved the sudden rising interest nationwide in the existence and powers of angels.

I have purposely omitted the name of the network program that aired this story, mainly because I felt that the flippant attitude of the reporters showed that they didn't take the story seriously, but rather felt it was just another scam or "it-takes-all-kinds-of-weirdos" affair. I, however, found the story highly interesting, informative, and thought-provoking. So much so that, being a writer, I decided to investigate further.

That same weekend I was scheduled to attend a reunion of veterans from my old military unit that served in Vietnam. At the reunion we exchanged war stories, some funny, some sad, and some I'd never heard before. We all agreed on one thing: We were the lucky ones. No sooner had someone said that than my friend Jack Weaver said, "We had the guardian angels with us, that's for sure."

Jack's words stayed with me for days after that. Try as I might, I could not forget what he had said, or the news show I had seen that same week. Jack had unknowingly given me an idea for my next book. I would explore aspects of wars and angels. But what did I know about angels? Then I suddenly realized that I was no stranger to this subject after all. For in my twenty-three years of military service, I had seen things happen in combat that defied all reason or logic and could be considered nothing short of miracles. How many others had witnessed similar events that could not be explained?

I found myself suddenly intrigued by the idea. It would require months of research, letter-writing, and phone calls. But those things are only minor challenges to the true writer. And besides, I already had one story—my own.

I do not profess to have ever seen an angel. Nor do I know anyone who has. The Reverend Billy Graham, a man many consider the greatest evangelist of our time, has stated that he has never seen an angel either, but has felt what he believes to be their presence at stressful times. Many people believe each and every one of us has a guardian angel. How many times have you narrowly averted a serious accident or mishap and heard someone say, "You must have a guardian angel watching over you?"

I immediately set about drafting an outline for this book. Angels! How hard could the research be? Everyone's heard about them, talked about them. There had to be tons of material on the subject. After all, there are nearly three hundred references to angels in the all-time best-seller, the Bible! So how difficult could this be?

Well, let me tell you, friends, people may have heard about them. They may talk about them. But very few people have ever written about them.

Without a doubt, the single most predominant book on this subject is *Angels: God's Secret Agents* by Billy Graham, published by Doubleday & Company. I highly recommend this book for anyone interested in learning more about angels.

I am greatly indebted to Dr. Graham for the insights provided by his outstanding book. It not only renewed my faith, which I regretfully admit had slid considerably over the last few years, but instilled within me a determination to search out every possible source I could find for my own book, in the hope that I could, in some small way, help resurrect people's belief and interest in God's messengers.

Certainly, if any group on this earth is in need of guidance and the protection of angels, it is the world's military personnel—men and women dedicated to the protection of their leaders, their people, and their country. Hailed as protectors of their nations, these men and women are delegated the awesome task of dealing with death and the threat of death every day. It is regrettable that the services of these men and women are still required in today's world. I am certain that they, as well as the rest of us who occupy this planet, wish it were not so. Unfortunately, as long as menacing evil walks among us, such armies and their services shall be necessary.

This book is dedicated to those who are committed to facing these problems and weapons of destruction on a daily basis. I hope that in reading about incidents that happened to many of their comrades-in-arms, they will be heartened by the fact that no matter what dark or desolate place in this troubled world in which they may find themselves, they are never truly alone.

# ANGELIC
# BATTLES

# 1
# Just What Are Angels?

BEFORE WE CAN VENTURE INTO THE STORIES OF ANGELS and their intervention into the lives of people, we must first do a little background examination of angels and how they are viewed around the world.

An angel is a spiritual being created by God. The word itself comes from the Greek word meaning "messenger." According to religious tradition, angels preside in heaven and act as God's servants and messengers between God and human beings. They also serve as guardians of individuals and nations.

Most religions include teachings about angels or similar beings. In some primitive religions, legends tell of bright, powerful spirits who appear in dreams and visions and protect people and tribes. In Hinduism and Buddhism, many major gods are accompanied by a band or court of spiritual beings.

Judaism, Christianity, and Islam have the most elaborate doctrines about angels. These religions recognize an order of beings in which angels rank above humans but below God.

The concept of angels with a corporal form and wings began in the Old Testament. Christian doctrine regarding angels reached full development in the twelfth and thirteenth centuries, especially in the teachings of St. Thomas Aquinas. Aquinas taught that countless numbers of angels existed and were immortal. They were necessary to fill the gap between God and the human race. According to Aquinas, angels knew everything except those things that depended on human choice and those things known only to God.

In 1667 the English poet John Milton strongly influenced the concept of angels with his famous epic *Paradise Lost,* which includes a version of Satan's fall from heaven and other Bible stories. Although over 326 years old, this is a story still well worth reading.

Regrettably, somewhere along the line the subject of angels disappeared. Was lost, if you will. Has our new, modern world become so high-tech that people no longer have an interest in such things? Have we advanced so far, so fast that we can no longer conceive of the possibility of another, spiritual world? That we live completely in the domain of the visible? That angels have now become only a myth?

How is it then that people have little or no problem believing in extraterrestrial visitors from other worlds? *Close Encounters of the Third Kind, E.T.,* and hundreds of other Hollywood productions fascinate us. We want to believe in such possibilities, yet many scoff the idea of angels. Why?

Despite the neglect of angels, we humans apparently cannot live without a belief in the existence of a spirit or spiritual world, a world where good and evil have a marked effect on humanity and history.

The purpose of this book is not to attempt to convert skeptics, atheists, or agnostics to the ways of the Lord. I will not battle the nonbelievers. For whatever reasons, they have elected to ignore the existence of a god, let alone angels. However, a Gallup Poll has revealed that 75 percent of Americans believe the devil exists and is a truly hideous creature who can strike fear into people. Now isn't that interesting? Many will not profess to believe in God or angels, yet have no problem believing in Satan. If you cannot believe in God, then you cannot believe in the Bible. If you cannot believe in the Bible, then how can you possibly believe in a devil and the powers of darkness? Interesting question, don't you think?

Well, there I go rambling on. I am not a clergyman, nor do I claim to be a Bible scholar. But these are questions I often ask when I encounter a nonbeliever. I shall, however, leave the attempted conversion of those who have not seen the light to more qualified individuals, such as Reverend Billy Graham and others who fight that battle every day.

The truth of guardian angels was never disputed in the earliest times of the Bible, or in the Middle Ages. As mentioned earlier, Christianity is not the only religion that believes in angels. Both Judaism and Islam have recorded many stories, superstitions, and legends about angels.

In my research into the accounts of individuals, I have found that the experience of guardian angels falls into five categories:

1. A personal appearance of a messenger or deliverer.

2. An unexplained audible voice.

3. A sudden surge of energy and strength.

4. A restraining influence.

5. An all-consuming inner warning of impending danger or peril.

Our purpose here is to examine angels, not in church, not in heaven, but rather in the trenches— the appearance or actions of a spiritual being whose intervention has meant the difference between life and death for an individual or group of individuals. Were the events actually divine acts by angels? You read the stories and you be the judge.

You are about to embark on a journey through time. Not a journey to heavenly places or through scenic gardens of scented beauty, but instead through periods of darkness, marked by wars, battles, and death brought about by the evil that still walks this universe today. For believers in the Bible, God, and His heavenly messengers, it shall at times prove a familiar journey, but one that shall confirm your faith and bring joy to your heart.

For the nonbeliever, I only ask that you withhold your judgment until we have reached our journey's end. Once you have put this book aside, maybe, just maybe, what you have read will uplift your spirit, give you a feeling that perhaps angels really are out there watching over all of us. Should you attain that feeling, pursue it. For if you can believe in angels, you are but one small step from knowing the greatest feeling in the world—belief in our Lord God . . .

## 2

# The Very First War

THE FIRST CONFLICT EVER RECORDED IN THIS UNIVERSE occurred not in Europe or the Middle East, but in heaven itself. It was a war that has not ended and it is fought every day. We are all part of that war, which began in the heavens and spread to the human race at the Garden of Eden. Its first mortal casualties were a man and woman named Adam and Eve. The combatants of that war are God and His angels, and their enemy Lucifer and the angels of darkness.

How could a war have happened in the most holy of places? How could there be rebellion in heaven? For the answers, we must refer to the only recorded words that describe the events leading up to this catastrophe that continues to this day.

This war was begun by Lucifer, one of the most beautiful and brilliant created beings in heaven, who is believed to be one of the archangels of God. Lucifer was known as the "son of the morning," created, as were all angels, for the purpose of glorifying God.

But Lucifer was not satisfied simply to serve his creator. He sought to rule over heaven and all creation. Considering himself the most beautiful being, his sense of pride overwhelming, he coveted the power that belongs to God.

Lucifer's high ambitions are exemplified in Isaiah 14:13–14: "I will ascend into heaven, I will exalt my throne above the stars of God: I will sit also upon the mount of the congregation . . . I will ascend above the heights of the clouds. I will be like the Most High."

As you can see, Lucifer coveted what was God's. He envisioned himself with total power over all that existed. Lucifer sought to be the one worshipped, not the one to do the worshipping. With him in his plot were nearly a third of the angels in heaven. Through his manipulation and scheming, he convinced them that his plan, although a daring one, could succeed. Thus Lucifer launched a rebellion against God and his faithful angels, who were led by the archangel Michael.

Revelations 12:7 provides the after-action report of that battle: "Then war broke out in heaven. Michael and his angels fought against the dragon [Lucifer], who fought back with his angels; but the dragon was defeated, and he and his angels were not allowed to stay in heaven any longer. The huge dragon was thrown out—that ancient serpent, named the Devil, or Satan, that deceived the whole world. He was cast down to earth, and all his angels with him"(GNB).

Although cast from heaven, Lucifer did not forgo his attempts to remove God from His rightful throne. The great Satan and his legions of darkness continue to bring misery and suffering to the human race. Through us Satan hopes to bring down his holy enemy. By creating wars, hatred, murder, and mayhem among those whom the Lord created and loves, Lucifer strikes blows into the heart of God and His angels.

We have only to look around us to see how well Satan is progressing with his evil agenda. Death, starvation, wars upon wars that seem to have no meaning or purpose, no ending. It is a war that has been waged since the dawn of history. Michael and his angels still battle the dragon at every turn; although we may not see the fight going on around us, it is there. And it will not end until that last great battle that will signal the last war in history. That war shall occur at a place called Armageddon, where it is foretold that Lucifer and his angels of darkness shall be destroyed forever.

Thus, the combatants of the very first war and the angels involved throughout time shall be the ones to fight this final battle. For those who believe, there is no doubt who the victor will be. For those who do not believe, if you never pray but one prayer in your life, save it for the day Michael and his angels arrive. I think you'll want to use it and a few hundred more before the day is over.

# 3

# Angels in the Old Testament

In my study of angels, I needed to refer to a book that I had allowed to lie long neglected in my home—the Bible. If you read the Bible from the first page to the last, you will find that it speaks of angels 273 times—108 times in the Old Testament and 165 times in the New Testament. To reject angels is to reject the Bible. A disbelief in these heavenly creatures, therefore, implies a disbelief in God Himself.

The angels in the Bible are referred to as a superhuman order of heavenly beings created by God, not gods in their own right. Exactly when they were created is unclear in the Bible. Many believe it was before the creation of the world. The following references apply.

Psalms 148:2–5: "Praise ye him, all his angels: praise ye him, all his hosts ... Let them praise the

name of the Lord: for he commanded, and they
were created.''

Paul in Colossians 1:16 states: ''For by him were
all things created, that are in heaven, and that are in
earth, visible and invisible, whether they be thrones,
or dominions, or principalities, or powers: all things
were created by him, and for him.''

Angels in the Old Testament are referred to by
other names as well: Abraham in Genesis 18:2 perceived them as ''three men.'' Jacob in Genesis 32:2
spoke of them as ''God's host.'' The Psalms referred
to them as ''the holy ones.'' In the book of Job they
are referred to as ''the sons of God.''

Purity, goodness, holiness, these are all attributes
we associate with angels. Indeed, if we are to believe
the Bible, they could not be conceived to be anything
else. In Genesis 1:31, God surveyed all His creation
and it was good; therefore angels were good.

The primary mission of God's angels is to serve
as a link between God and human beings. Both the
Old Testament and the New Testament contain numerous stories of angels watching over true believers
and protecting their interests. However, belief in
guardian angels is not an explicit teaching of the
Bible. The Holy Bible does, however, leave little
doubt as to the validity of such guardians: ''The
angel of the Lord encampeth round about them that
fear him, and delivereth them'' (Psalms 34:7). ''For
he shall give his angels charge over thee, to keep
thee in all thy ways'' (Psalms 91:11).

Perhaps the most well-known story of the Old Testament is contained in the book of Exodus. It is a
story of a simple people confronting one of the most
powerful armies of the time. Even if you have never
read a single verse from the Bible, the odds are that

you know this story as well as any Bible scholar. For it is the story of Moses (Charlton Heston to non–Bible readers who have seen the movie *The Ten Commandments*) and how he was chosen to lead the people of Israel out of bondage from the pharaoh of Egypt. It is a powerful story of two strong-willed men, one, Moses, drawn to a burning bush on a mountain by an angel of the Lord, the other, the pharaoh of Egypt, king over all he surveyed, a man who sought to keep enslaved the Lord's chosen people of Israel.

Although the events of this story may not be considered a war as we know it, it was a war of wills, and had the deadly consequences of wars that have come and gone through the centuries: suffering, death, a winner and loser. Where the pharaoh used his powerful army, Moses used only the power of God and His angels. Needless to say, the pharaoh was outgunned from the start; he just didn't know it.

Even when God's powers were demonstrated to the pharaoh, he scoffed at Moses and refused to let Moses' people go. Plagues were cast down upon Egypt, and still he refused. Not until the Lord sent His angel of death to slay the firstborn of all Egypt did pharaoh finally release his hold on Moses' people and set them free.

Following the angel of the Lord, Moses led his people out of Egypt. When they reached the Red Sea, they rested.

Back in Egypt, the pharaoh's heart was hardened against Moses and the Israelites and he sought revenge for the loss of his own firstborn. Marshaling his forces, he set out in pursuit of the Israelites, intent on slaying them in great numbers to show his power. But God had already warned Moses of the pharaoh's actions and told him not to fear. For this would be the last time the Israelites would have to cast their eyes upon the soldiers of Egypt.

As the Egyptians bore down on the Israelites, who had their backs to the sea, Moses stretched forth his staff and divided the waters of the Red Sea, providing an escape route for the children of Israel. The pharaoh's bitterness toward Moses blinded him to the miracle he witnessed before him. With rage and hatred overflowing in his heart, he ordered his army of over six hundred chariots into the opened sea and continued his pursuit of Moses.

It was the last ever seen of the pharaoh's mighty army. From the other shore, Moses, obeying God's voice, raised his hand and moved it across the waters, causing the sea to come together again, drowning the Egyptian army.

This shortened version of this great story does not do it justice by any means. For those who have never read the entire story, I highly recommend it. For those who say you never have the time, I recommend the movie *The Ten Commandments*—without a doubt, one of the greatest movies of all time, is both entertaining and accurate.

# 4
# The Angel in the Fiery Furnace

IN THE BOOK OF DANIEL WE FIND ANOTHER STORY THAT emphasizes the power of guardian angels, set in the time of the Babylonian and Persian empires, when Jews suffered greatly from persecution and oppression, but their faith in their God did not waver.

King Nebuchadnezzar had his minions construct a golden statue ninety feet high and nine feet wide and place it on the plain of Dura, in the province of Babylon. He then ordered all officials of the province to gather there to pay homage to his god. Once the music began for the dedication, all would bow to the golden statue. Any who refused would be cast into a fiery furnace. Shadrach, Meshach, and Abednego, Jewish officials in the province of Babylon, refused. Noting this, their enemies saw the opportunity to rid themselves of the three men they despised.

Hurrying to Nebuchadnezzar, they told of the three men's refusal to bow as the king instructed. The King flew into a rage and ordered the three brought before him, then asked if what he had been told was true. Had they refused to bow to his golden god? They admitted that they would not bow to a golden statue.

This posed a problem for the king. These men were friends of the king's trusted adviser Daniel and officials in the province of Babylon. In the hope that they might have changed their minds now that they were in the palace, the king asked the musicians to play again so that the three could now bow and all would be forgotten. But once again, the three refused, saying, "We do not fear. For our God will send forth his angel to protect us, for it is only in Him that we believe."

The king, his patience stretched to the limit, lost his temper. His face turned red with anger and he leaped to his feet, screaming for his guards to heat the furnace seven times hotter than it had ever been before. He then commanded the strongest men in his army to tie up the three men and throw them into the blazing furnace.

The guards reacted immediately. Grabbing the three fully-clothed men, they threw them to the floor and secured them tightly with rope, then carried them to the furnace.

Because the king had given strict orders that the furnace be heated to seven times its normal heat, the guards assigned to carry out the king's orders were consumed by the fire themselves as they tossed Shadrach, Meshach, and Abednego into the heart of the fiery blaze.

Expecting to hear the screams of his victims, the king suddenly leaped to his feet and shouted to his officials, "Did we not bind three men and cast them into the blazing furnace?"

"We did, Your Majesty," they answered.

"Then why is it that I now see four men walking about in the fire?" asked the king. "They are not bound, and they show no sign of pain—and the fourth one looks like a god."

No one in the room could provide the king with the answer to these questions. So Nebuchadnezzar went to the door of the furnace and called out, "Shadrach! Meshach! Abednego! Servants of the supreme God! Come out!"

The three men emerged from the fiery furnace at once as instructed. The king and all his officials gathered around them and witnessed that neither their clothes nor their hair was singed, nor was there even the smell of smoke about them. The witnesses were truly amazed at this wonder, especially the king, who proclaimed, "Praise the God of Shadrach, Meshach, and Abednego! He sent His angel and rescued these men who serve and trust Him."

# 5
# *Daniel and the Angel*

DANIEL, A SON OF A NOBLE ISRAELITE FAMILY, HAD been chosen by King Nebuchadnezzar to serve in the royal court. Those selected had to be handsome, intelligent, well-trained, quick to learn, and free of any physical defect. Daniel easily fulfilled these requirements. He was exceptionally bright and was in favor with God. And no matter what question the king asked or what problem arose within the kingdom, Daniel always knew ten times more than any fortune-teller or magician in the king's court. This endeared Daniel to the King.

With the passing of Nebuchadnezzar, Daniel found himself serving the new king, Darius the Mede, who had seized power by killing the son of Nebuchadnezzar. Darius was no fool. He had witnessed the wisdom of Daniel and chose him as one of the supervisors of the provincial governors who looked after the new king's interests.

Daniel, in his usual way, soon showed that he

could handle the affairs of the kingdom much more efficiently than the governors and other advisers. Soon Darius began to consider making Daniel the chief administrator over the entire empire. Of course, this did not set well with the governors or the other court advisers. They plotted to discredit Daniel and rid themselves of him once and for all. But this proved easier said than done. For Daniel was reliable and intelligent, and did not do anything wrong or dishonest.

They met one night and said, "We are not going to find anything of which to accuse Daniel unless it is something in connection with his religion." So they went to the king and convinced him that because he was the all-powerful ruler, he should issue an order that for thirty days no one be permitted to request anything from any god or from any man except the king. Anyone who disobeyed this order would be cast into the lions' den. Darius was well into his sixties, and these men played upon his vanity and convinced the old man that this order would be truly a great sign of his strength and power over the empire.

After hearing that the king had signed the order, Daniel went home. In an upstairs room were windows that faced toward Jerusalem. Just as he had always done three times a day, Daniel knelt at the open windows and prayed. This was the opportunity his enemies had been waiting for. They immediately rushed to the king and informed on Daniel, stating that he was in direct violation of the king's order and must suffer the consequences as prescribed by the king. Daniel must be cast into the lions' den.

Darius was in a terrible predicament. He truly liked Daniel and knew of the man's honesty and loyalty to all he had served. The king told the accusers to leave and return at dusk, at which time he would make his decision.

For hours the king struggled to find some way to rescue Daniel from this situation, but he could not. By Medes and Persian law, no order, once signed by the king, could be changed. So he ordered Daniel to the palace. With Daniel's enemies present, the king told Daniel that he was to be cast into the lions' den. The king concluded, "May your God, whom you have served so loyally, rescue you."

Daniel was cast into the pit and a huge stone was positioned over it. The king's royal seal was placed on the stone so that no one could rescue Daniel. Then the king returned to the palace for what was to be a long and sleepless night.

At dawn the king hurried to the pit and called out anxiously, "Daniel, servant of the living God! Was the God you serve so loyally able to save you from the lions?"

Daniel replied, "May Your Majesty live forever! God sent forth his angel to shut the mouths of the lions so that they would not hurt me. He did this because he knew I was innocent and because I have not wronged you, Your Majesty."

The king was overjoyed and had Daniel removed from the pit. Then the king had Daniel's accusers cast into the pit, where they were devoured almost immediately by the hungry lions.

Daniel went on to prosper during the reign of Darius.

# 6

# *Angels in the New Testament*

IN CAESAREA, CORNELIUS, A ROMAN ARMY CAPTAIN IN what was called the Italian regiment, was a religious man; he and his entire family worshipped God. He did much to help the poor of Jewish descent and prayed often.

One afternoon while praying, he had a vision in which he clearly saw an angel of the Lord come down and say to him, "Cornelius, God is pleased with your works of charity and with your prayers, and is ready to answer you. Send to Joppa for a man whose name is Simon Peter. He is in the home of a leathermaker named Simon, who lives by the sea." Then the angel departed.

The Roman captain sent two servants and a soldier to find Peter. By the time they arrived at the leathermakers' house, Simon Peter had already been told by another angel that they were coming and that he was to go with them. Although not fully understanding the message, Peter went to the house of Cornelius with the escort.

The following day, Cornelius described the vision he had experienced and asked Peter the meaning of the visitation. Peter explained the Jewish belief in God. During his explanation, "The Holy Spirit came down on all those who were listening to his message." Seeing that the Romans had received the Holy Spirit, Peter then ordered them baptized in the name of Jesus Christ.

When word of Romans being baptized spread throughout the land, a great uproar arose from both Jews and Romans alike. King Herod had James, the brother of John the Baptist, arrested and put to the sword. He then sent out his soldiers to arrest Peter and bring him to the palace prison. There he was handed over to four groups of four guards who were to watch over him constantly until after his public trial and execution.

The night before Herod was to bring Peter before the people for his public trial, Peter was sleeping between Roman guards. He was tied with two chains, and more soldiers guarded the door of the cell and the gates of the prison.

Suddenly an angel appeared. He stood before the door of Peter's cell, illuminating it. The angel woke Peter and said, "Hurry! Get up!" At once the chains fell from Peter's hands. Then the angel said, "Tighten your belt and put on your sandals."

Peter did as he was told. The angel said, "Put your cloak around you and come with me." Peter followed him out of the prison. They passed by the first and second guard stations, where the guards

were awake and alert but did not see Peter or the
angel. They came at last to the iron gate that led into
the city. As they neared the gate, it opened by itself,
and they went out. They walked down the street, and
suddenly the angel was gone.

Then Peter realized what had happened and said,
"Now I know that it is really true! The Lord sent
his angel to rescue me from Herod's power and from
everything the Jewish people expected to happen to
me."

# 7
# John's Visions of Revelation

JUST AS THE STORY OF MOSES IS ONE OF THE BEST-known of the Old Testament, John's writings at the end of the New Testament are also known throughout the world.

Nowhere in the Bible are there more references to the angels of God than in the book of Revelation. It is a book that is as frightening as it is interesting to read. Although there are differences of opinion regarding the interpretation of this book, the central theme is clear: There will come a time when the Lord God will finally and totally defeat all His enemies, including the evil Satan and his corps of fallen angels. When this has come to pass, God shall reward the faithful with the blessings of a new heaven and a new earth.

The book of Revelation is a record of the events that Jesus Christ revealed to his servant John through an angel, with instructions to tell all of what he saw and what had been prophesied. To evaluate fully the entire book of Revelation would take considerable time and cause considerable disagreement among readers, and since this book is to be about angels rather than a detailed study of the Bible, I have selected a few passages to demonstrate what John saw and heard in regard to angels. This by no means is meant to lessen the importance of the book of Revelation and its crystal-clear theme. I encourage all readers to take a few moments from their busy lives to read the writings of John and the wonders he reportedly encountered.

John's story was written, as was much of the Bible, at a time when Christians were being persecuted because of their faith in Jesus Christ as the Lord. After being arrested for his preaching, John was found guilty and sent to the island of Patmos to isolate him and keep him from spreading his religion. There one day the spirit took control of him and he heard a loud voice that sounded like a trumpet, speaking behind him. The voice told him to "write down all that you are about to see, and send the book to the churches of seven cities."

Startled by this sudden voice, John turned to see who was speaking and saw seven golden lampstands, and what looked like a man, wearing a robe that reached to his feet and a gold band around his chest. His hair was as white as wool and his eyes blazed like fire; his feet shone like brass and his voice sounded like a waterfall. He held seven stars in his right hand, and a sharp two-edged sword came out of his mouth. His face was as bright as the midday sun.

John fell to the ground at the feet of this vision, truly frightened by the sight before him. The robed figure reached out and touched him, saying, "Do not be afraid, John, for you have been chosen to write all the things you will see, both the things that are now and the things that are to come.''

After John had written all that was to be sent to the seven churches, he had another vision and saw a door open in heaven. A voice called to him, ''Come up here, and I will show you what must happen after the churches have received my words.''

In heaven was a throne with someone sitting on it. His face gleamed like precious stones, and all around the throne was a rainbow the color of emeralds. In the circle around the throne were twenty-four other thrones on which were seated twenty-four elders dressed in white and wearing crowns of gold.

John saw a scroll in the right hand of the one who sat on the throne; it was covered with writing on both sides and was sealed with seven seals. A mighty angel announced in a loud voice, ''Who is worthy to break the seals and open the scroll?'' Then John saw a lamb standing in the center of the throne. The lamb went forward and took the scroll from the right hand of the one on the throne.

(During the events leading to the tragedy in Waco that ended in the death of David Koresh and some of his followers, Koresh told the FBI that he would surrender once he had transcribed the meaning of the seven seals of revelations—the same seven seals of which John wrote so long ago.)

John watched as the lamb broke open the first of the seven seals. And there came forth a rider holding a bow, on a white horse. The rider was given a crown and rode out as a conqueror.

Then the second seal was broken and a red horse appeared. Its rider was given a large sword and the power to bring war upon the earth, so that people could kill each other.

The third seal brought a rider on a black horse. He held a pair of scales high in his hand by which to measure fairness.

Then the lamb broke open the fourth seal and John shuddered, for now a pale-colored horse rode in. Its rider's name was Death, and Hades followed close behind. He was given authority over one-fourth of the earth, to kill by means of war, famine, disease, and wild animals.

The fifth seal was broken and John saw underneath the altar the souls of those who had died for proclaiming God's word and had been faithful in their witnessing for the Lord. Each had been given a white robe, and when they asked the Lord how long they must wait before God punished those who had killed them, they were told to be patient and to rest awhile longer, for the judgment day was coming soon.

At the opening of the sixth seal, there came a great earthquake and the sun became as black as coarse black cloth and the moon turned as red as blood. The stars fell to the earth. The sky disappeared like a scroll being rolled up, and every mountain and island was moved from its place. Then kings of the earth, the rulers and the military chiefs, the rich and the powerful, and all other people, slave and free, fled for the caves to hide themselves from the eyes of the one who sat on the throne.

After this, John saw four angels standing at the four corners of the earth, holding back the four winds so that no wind should blow on the earth or the sea or against any tree. And he saw another angel coming up from the east with the seal of the living God in his hand. He called out in a loud voice to the four angels whom God had given the power to damage the earth and the sea and said, "Do not harm the earth, the sea, or the trees until we mark the servants of our God with a seal on their foreheads."

When the lamb broke open the seventh seal there was a long silence in heaven. Then John saw the seven angels who stood before God, and they were given seven trumpets.

Another angel came forward with a gold incense container and stood before the altar. The smoke of the burning incense went up with prayers of God's people from the hands of the angel. Then the angel took the incense container, filled it with fire from the altar, and cast it down upon the earth. There were rumblings and peals of thunder, flashes of lightning, and an earthquake.

Without a doubt, John saw more angels than any other prophet in the Bible. And the passages related are by no means the complete text of the book of Revelation. John still encountered the angel and the little scroll, the three angels spreading the word, the seven angels with the last plagues, and the final defeat of Satan.

# THE
# CIVIL WAR

THE CIVIL WAR WAS ONE OF THE DARKEST TIMES IN American history. It was a war that set brother against brother, father against son, and neighbor against neighbor. The conflict was brought about by the political question of states' rights and the moral question of one's right to own another. Thousands died before these questions were resolved and changed the course of a nation.

Although well-documented for its time, the Civil War proved to be one of the more difficult periods of my research in regard to angelic or unexplained spiritual occurrences. I believe there were such happenings, but writing or discussing them in that time period would undoubtedly have meant a one-way ticket to the nearest home for the mentally "touched."

I did manage to locate two highly interesting stories, thanks largely to the efforts of the research staff at Oklahoma University, to whom I owe a debt of gratitude for not only these, but a number of other stories in this book.

# 8

# Mother Bickerdyke's Guardian Angel

*For he shall give his angels charge over thee, to keep thee in all thy ways.*

—PSALMS 91:11

TO MANY, MARY BICKERDYKE WAS HERSELF AN ANGEL. She was born in July 1817 on a small farm in Ohio, to a mother who died when Mary was only seventeen months old. Raising a child proved too much for her father, and soon she was being passed from relative to relative. By her teen years she had developed an interest in medicine, but lack of education and the inability of women to attend medical schools at that time soon dampened any hope of pursuing that vocation.

By the age of twenty she had met and married a

man twice her age who had several children from a first marriage. Mary proved to be a good wife and mother, bearing two fine, healthy sons. Later she had a daughter, but little Martha died when she was only two. In her sadness, Mary Bickerdyke wondered if she might have saved her daughter had she only known more about medicine.

With the death of her husband in 1859, she found herself the sole support of her children and stepchildren. She took up the study of botanic medicine, therapy that used drugs made of vegetable juices, bark, roots, and herbs. Highly competent and self-taught, Mary had already gained the respect of the community for her skills as a nurse when the Civil War started.

On a warm Sunday not long after the war began, Mary sat in her regular seat at the Galesburg Congregational Church, but on this day the Reverend Edward Beecher chose to forgo his normal sermon. Having returned only a few days earlier from the Union camp at Cairo, Illinois, he began to describe the terrible conditions he had witnessed and the neglect of the young Illinois soldiers suffering from typhoid and dysentery. Conditions for Illinois fighting men were deplorable, he said sadly. Something had to be done. By the time he finished, the congregation had vowed to provide some relief for the army of Illinois.

To Mary Bickerdyke, it seemed more than just money was necessary. What those boys needed was someone to care for them, someone who knew medicine. Someone like Mary.

Leaving her children in the care of the congregation, Mary set out on what she felt was her God-chosen mission.

Arriving at her first camp, she immediately saw the cause of the deplorable conditions. The stench could be smelled a mile away. The men hadn't bothered to dig trenches for latrines, but instead used the surrounding woods. The water was understandably filthy. On one side of the camp were mountains of garbage. She noted the carcasses of a number of dead dogs among the souring piles. The rancid odor of frying grease used over and over fouled what little clean air escaped the putrid garbage.

However, these sickening sights, as disgusting as they were, were nothing compared to what Mary found as she approached the aid station; piled nearly as high as the garbage were the amputated arms and legs of the unfortunate wounded.

Horrified, Mary first chastised Union surgeons, then turned her wrath upon the camp commander. Admiring the woman's spunk, the commander remained calm during her scolding and waited patiently until Mary had finished before replying, "If you think you can do better, then have at it, little lady."

Placing an entire company of Union soldiers at her disposal, the commander informed them that an order from Mary was the same as an order from him. Never one to idle away time, Mary set about her work with the skill of a well-versed veteran first sergeant. Latrines were dug and orders were posted for the men to use them. The garbage, the dead dogs, and the amputated limbs were buried, and disposal holes were dug for future use. Next she brought on the wrath of the cooks by insisting that the grease used for cooking be carried into the woods and dumped into trenches every night and that dishes be washed in hot water after every meal, not simply rinsed in cold water.

Within a week, the smell that had hung over the camp like a plague was gone. The air was clean and fresh once more and the morale of the camp improved one hundred percent—especially on those evenings when Mary herself would do the cooking.

And so it was that Mary Bickerdyke began her work, moving from camp to camp to do what she could. Once a camp was sanitized, she ministered to the wounded, getting them out of their filthy, bloody clothes, bathing them, then boiling their towels and underclothes. Much of her time was spent giving medicines and, more often, holding a trembling hand or stroking a dying young boy's hair until the end came. Soon Mary Bickerdyke became known as Mother Bickerdyke, mother to the wounded.

Mary's efficiency and hard work did not go unnoticed by the soldiers and officers with whom she came in contact. Eventually she served as the superintendent of the hospital in Cairo. Following Union victories in Tennessee, Mother Bickerdyke was asked to serve as matron of the military hospital in Memphis.

As she had done since her arrival at the first Union camp, Mary Bickerdyke charged headlong into her newly acquired task. Orderlies who thought they could stay out of the frontline fighting by working at the hospital quickly discovered that their leisurely daily routine of sitting around smoking, playing cards, and drinking while wounded soldiers cared for sicker comrades was about to come to a sudden halt.

In a fiery speech to the staff, Mary made it perfectly clear that any orderly who wished to continue in his lackluster ways would be immediately reported to the Union commander and sent to the front lines, where she felt certain General Lee and his forces could provide enough shot and shell to allow little time for folly such as smoking, drinking, and card playing. The choice was theirs. Needless to say, efficiency and patient care improved overnight.

A more pressing problem that interfered with Mary's operation of the hospital was dealing with corrupt officers, especially medical officers. Men of few values or honor, they saw the opportunity to line their pockets at the expense of a nation's suffering soldiers.

Mary Bickerdyke was a civilian and held no official rank in the military. Issuing orders to privates was one thing, but directing high-ranking officers was another thing all together. Not a woman to be tolerant of incompetence or corrupt authority, Mother Mary had a number of openly hostile encounters with those who sought to profit from the war.

Once, when a requisition for much-needed medical supplies and drugs for newly arrived wounded was denied, Mary openly defied the corrupt quartermaster's orders and, with the aid of a small group of her armed orderlies, forced her way into a warehouse and secured the items she needed. Seeing the supplies arrive at the hospital, one of the doctors who had been party to the quartermaster's plan to resell the supplies shouted in a loud and indignant voice, "Woman! Who gave the authority to take those supplies?"

Mary disembarked from her wagon, then climbed up the steps of the hospital until she was standing toe to toe with her adversary to demonstrate that she would not be intimidated. She addressed the arrogant doctor in a voice loud enough for all to hear. "I receive my authority from God! Do you have anyone ranking higher than that, Doctor?"

Midway through the third year of the war, Mother Bickerdyke's fame had spread far and wide. Listed among her friends were Generals Ulysses S. Grant and William T. Sherman, as well as a number of congressmen and senators.

Never one to stay in one place too long, she was with Grant at Vicksburg, helping to organize a nursing corps that saved the lives of thousands of wounded soldiers during that long, bitter siege. Mary was the only woman present at the battles of Lookout Mountain and Missionary Ridge.

At Missionary Ridge Mother Bickerdyke's fame gained new status. Working feverishly at an aid station just behind the battle lines, Mary overheard two wounded soldiers asking a stretcher bearer about another comrade who had fallen near them and rolled into a small ravine. Had they found him? Whether from fatigue or fear, the orderly barked back, "Hell, man, how do I know! If we didn't get him, then forget it—he's good as dead. Sun'll be goin' down soon, and ain't nobody goin' out on that battlefield in the dark, less'n they wanta get their fool head blowed off."

Mary was troubled. The thought of wounded lying undiscovered under brush or thickets or in a ravine haunted her as she watched the sun set and darkness begin to fall over the battlefield. Approaching the stretcher bearers, she asked for volunteers to go out with her and search for any wounded who might have been overlooked. They refused, assuring her that all that remained out there were the dead.

Having little faith in what the men told her, Mary returned to the two wounded soldiers she had heard earlier. They provided her with the approximate distance and a detailed description of the area where they had last seen their fallen comrade.

Proceeding to her tent, Mary secured a lantern, checked that it had enough fuel, and lit it. Its glow reflected on her Bible lying on a makeshift nightstand next to her cot. Placing her hand on the Holy Book, she said, ''Oh, Lord, I am about to venture into the valley of death. I ask that you, in all your graciousness, protect me as I go in search of your injured children. In God's name, I ask. Amen.''

Moving outside the camp, she was stopped by one of the young pickets on guard duty. When she told him what she intended to do, the soldier immediately tried to discourage her from her mission. He knew the area she was talking about. He had seen the ravine, but the Rebel lines were too close to it now. ''You can't wander about out there with a lit lantern, Mother Bickerdyke. The Rebs got sharpshooters all along them woods and up in the rocks. They'll shoot you dead for sure before you can get anywhere near that ravine. You better stay here.''

Mary would not be denied. ''There is a wounded boy out there who needs me. The good Lord has been with me through this war and I see no reason to lose faith in Him now. Have no fear, boy. I will not be walking alone.''

The young soldier, seeing her determination, began calling for the sergeant-of-the-guard. As he did so, Mary smiled and walked beyond the picket line and was soon on the battlefield. A crowd of Union soldiers quickly gathered along the picket line as the word spread. Although they could barely make out her figure, the lantern was clearly visible in every direction. Many of the Union troops began to pray, but none made a move to follow after her.

As she threaded her way among the dead, the glow of the light reflected off uniforms of blue and gray alike. Mary uttered a prayer for those who had departed for a better place. For them, the pain and suffering of the cruel war was over.

As she neared the ravine, the men on the Union lines stared in stunned amazement as the light surrounding Mother Bickerdyke suddenly brightened to three times the normal strength of the lantern. It seemed to envelop her in a soft golden glow.

At that same instant, three shots rang out from the woods along the Rebel lines at a distance of no more than fifty yards. All three shots fell short, hitting at the base of the light that surrounded the woman of mercy.

Mary stood perfectly still, whether from fear or a strong sense of security, she herself was never quite sure. Another volley echoed on the heels of the first with the same results; incredibly, the renowned Southern marksmen missed the target again.

Before another shot could be fired, a Rebel officer galloped forward. Immediately recognizing the figure in the field, he began to shout, "Stop firing! Stop firing! That's Mother Bickerdyke!"

The woods fell silent for a moment, then a voice from the Rebel lines called out to her, "You must have the angels with you tonight, Mother Bickerdyke. The field is yours, madam—and God bless you."

Mary moved forward. As she did so, the lantern returned to its normal glow. Searching for only a moment, she found the wounded soldier exactly where his comrades had said he would be. Although weak from loss of blood, the boy managed to gain his feet, and Mary led him back to the Union lines, to the cheers of both blue and gray alike.

What miracle had saved Mary Bickerdyke from the eagle-eyed marksmanship of not one but three expert riflemen? They were men who were accustomed to hitting targets at distances of over two hundred yards with deadly accuracy, yet had missed at fifty yards. How does one explain a lantern magnifying its power three times its normal strength at the same instant that shots are being fired—shots that fail to penetrate that light?

Here we have a simple country girl and self-taught nurse who managed to survive some of the most horrific battles of the Civil War amid thousands of bullets and flying shrapnel from cannon fire, who never once received as much as a single scratch from those encounters. If indeed there are guardian angels, then this lady's was working overtime. But then strong faith can and often does work miracles.

Following the war, Mary was given an honored place with Sherman's troops in the great victory parade of May 24, 1865, held in Washington, D.C. She became friends with famed poet Walt Whitman, who himself had nursed the wounded at Union hospitals. She continued her work with a war charity organization that would later become better known as the Red Cross.

Mary served in the war from June 9, 1861, to March 20, 1865. She was in nineteen hard-fought battles, saving the lives of countless soldiers on both sides.

Age and years of hard work and dedication finally caught up with Mary. As she lay dying of pneumonia, she granted a reporter's request to speak to her. He asked how she had found the courage to walk the battlefields at night with a lantern.

She smiled and answered, "From that very first night, I knew that I was never alone. For God's angels walked beside me on hallowed ground."

Did this woman of so much compassion, caring, and commitment walk the night with her guardian angel? You be the judge.

# 9

# An Angel in the Wilderness

*But if these beings guard you, they do so because they have been summoned by your prayers.*

—St. AMBROSE

THE DATE IS MAY 5, 1864. THE PLACE IS A DARK woodland south of the Rapidan River, ten miles west of Fredericksburg, Pennsylvania. The area is known as the Wilderness, a forbidding woodland consisting of impenetrable tangled underbrush, dense woods, gullies, streams, and a handful of clearings. There are few roads through the area and most of them are mere wagon track paths that hamper adequate passage of large wagon trains or troop movements. The only good passages around this entanglement of woods and brush is the Orange Turnpike to the north and the Orange Plank Road to the south.

In this wilderness, over five thousand men will lose their lives over the next two days. The wounded will number over fifteen thousand, and the missing will be tallied at over four thousand. It is a place that will be remembered by both Yankees and Rebels as a hell on earth.

On the morning of the fifth, Generals Ulysses S. Grant and George Gordon Meade were notified that Confederate forces under General Richard Stoddert Ewell were moving on the Orange Turnpike; thinking the force to be only a division, Grant ordered an attack. Union forces under General Gouverner Warren engaged the Confederate force, an encounter that soon escalated into a full-fledged battle. Grant soon realized that the Confederate troops were not a minor element of General Robert E. Lee's army, but the main force itself.

Because of the thick woods, the men were often firing at one another at point-blank range. Battle lines became confused in the smoke-filled woods; regiments lost contact with one another. Commanders led their men by following the sounds of firing, often finding themselves shooting at each other or at the muzzle flashes of an enemy they could not see.

To add to the confusion, Confederate General A. P. Hill began to advance with his forces up the Orange Plank Road to the south. There he was met by Union General Winfield Scott Hancock, and a separate and equally desperate battle ensued. Again the battle was fought at close quarters, often hand-to-hand, with bayonets and rifles used as clubs. All day the fighting surged back and forth, with ground being taken, held for an hour, lost in a counterattack, then retaken. As evening fell, nothing significant had been gained by either side, and the forces retired to whatever makeshift lines they could form before darkness fell.

Grateful for the opportunity at last to get some rest, men from both sides of the bloody conflict soon found that even the darkness would not allow them to escape the suffering and misery that had marked the day's terrible events. A new enemy now unleashed its wrath upon the wounded and dying who lay in the tangles and wood-choked gullies of the confusing battlefield. The new enemy was fire.

In the bitter fighting just before dark, the musket flashes had started a number of small fires that now erupted into a full-fledged forest fire. Caught in the path of the blaze were the dead and wounded of both armies who were strewn all through the woods. Soon the magnitude of the situation became fully known as men screamed in agonizing pain when the flames began to consume the wounded. Piercing cries and pleas for death echoed through the darkness. The air began to fill with the smell of burning flesh. It was more than even these hardened veterans could stand.

Sergeant William Neil of the 27th Virginia Regiment of the famed Stonewall Brigade went to his commander, Lieutenant Colonel Charles L. Haynes, and requested that the colonel attempt to arrange a truce so that both sides might join to remove the wounded from the path of the fire. The colonel agreed and told the sergeant to organize volunteers for the dangerous task while he made arrangements with Union forces holding the positions across from them.

Among the Virginia volunteers was a young Rebel soldier named Joshua Bates, the son of a Baptist minister who had disowned his only son for engaging in this awful war.

The truce arranged, Sergeant Neil and ten volunteers put their weapons aside and went to meet a

Union sergeant and ten of his unarmed men in a clearing between the lines. The two squads braved the heat and the flames of the forest fire to bring out their wounded brothers in arms, without regard to the color of their uniforms.

The mission of mercy continued for over an hour, with the wounded hastily carried back to the clearing, where others tended them and moved them farther back behind the lines. But even with this effort, not all could be rescued. The screams of the less fortunate carried on the night air filled with smoke, heat, and the smell of burning meat. Still the rescuers returned time after time in an effort to save as many as possible from such a terrible death.

Weary from running back and forth and suffering from near heat exhaustion, Private Bates and three others returned once more into the flames to retrieve a soldier screaming that his pants were on fire. Locating the man, Bates dropped to his knees and threw dirt onto the burning pants to put out the fire.

As the rescuers prepared to pick up the wounded man, they heard a loud cracking sound and saw a towering tree in all its fiery glory crash down between them and the only way out of the fire. The rescuers themselves were now surrounded by the roaring blaze that quickly began to close in on them. There were no avenues of escape, and any hope of rescue was impossible. One of the soldiers cried out, "My God . . . we're all going to die!"

Kneeling beside the wounded soldier, Private Bates encouraged those around him to join hands as he prayed.

"Oh, Lord, our task this night has been a mighty one. We have risked all to save our fellow man. Would you now reward us for showing compassion

by committing us to this fiery furnace? We beseech
you, Almighty God . . . come to our aid in this time
of great need. In your name, we ask. Amen.''

From their tightly knit group within the surrounding flames, the four men saw a lone figure appear beyond the fire. It was a figure of unusual
height, dressed not in a uniform but in what appeared
to be a white sackcloth robe. The figure raised a
hand and called to the men surrounded by the flames,
''Come out, hurry! Come this way and bring your
wounded brother.''

Hesitant at first, the men looked at one another,
then back to the figure who now seemed to move
directly into the flames, yet was unharmed by the
fire. Again the calm and gentle voice told them to
follow him. Still uncertain, but having little to lose,
the four men picked up the wounded soldier and
began moving toward the figure in the fire. As they
neared the flames the figure turned and walked away.
As it did, a sudden wind swept over the men and the
wall of flame seem to split apart, leaving an opening
of some twenty feet. Without delay, Bates and the
others hurried through the exit. Within seconds they
were free of the raging fire that immediately consumed the very area in which they had been kneeling
only minutes before.

Scurrying clear of the heat and flames, the men
placed the wounded man on the ground and looked
around for the figure who had encouraged them to
escape certain death, but no one was there. They
were the only ones in the immediate area. The mysterious figure had vanished.

In a letter to his parents following the battle of the
Wilderness, young Joshua Bates told of what had
happened that night in the fiery woods, of how two

armies at war had put aside their differences for a time to save not a Yankee or a Rebel, but their fellow man. Bates was convinced that his prayer for their rescue had been answered by the intervention of one of God's angels on that night.

Bates's father was so moved by the experience related by his son that he read the letter to the congregation of his church before beginning his sermon one Sunday morning. He then immediately went home and wrote to his only son, the first letter he had written since Joshua went off to war.

Private Nathan Riddle, a member of the Union's 19th Massachusetts, was with Bates that night and likewise wrote of the experience to his parents in Boston. Although not a highly religious man, Riddle could not explain the events of that night, other than to suggest that there had to have been some type of divine intervention.

Could it have been an angel who came in answer to Joshua Bates's prayer? Was escape from certain death their reward for the goodness and kindness they showed toward their fellow man?

Bates survived the Civil War and returned home, where he became a Baptist preacher and was often requested to relate his story of the miracle that had occurred in the bloody battle of the Wilderness. He passed away quietly in his sleep in December 1913, convinced that his life had been spared that night by an angel of the Lord.

Sergeant William Neil, who had organized the rescue volunteers, was later killed at the battle of Cold Harbor.

Private Nathan Riddle was seriously wounded at the battle of Spotsylvania only a few weeks after the Wilderness battle. His left arm had to be amputated.

After returning home to Boston, he became a school-teacher and avid supporter of his local church, often relating the story of that night to any who would listen. He died at the age of seventy-six, likewise convinced that what happened in the woods of the Wilderness was far above anything mortal man could explain.

# THE
# INDIAN WARS

*Around our pillows, golden ladders rise,*
*And up and down the skies,*
*With winged sandals shod,*
*The Angels come and go, the messengers of God!*

   —R. H. Stoddard, "Hymn to the Beautiful"

While searching through literally hundreds of books, magazines, and newspapers dealing with angel lore during wartime, I came upon an interesting yet far from honorable time in our past. Many called it manifest destiny. Others preferred the word "progress." However, no matter what term or phrase is used, the end result always remains the same. During this period of our history, we—the great humanitarians—attempted to rape, plunder, and kill, in mass quantities, an entire people for the want of what they had—land. Had sanity and reason not prevailed when it did, we possibly would have succeeded in the annihilation of an entire race of noble people, the American Indian.

Now before you say, "Wait a minute. Indians

didn't know anything about angels!'' let's take a closer look at Indian beliefs and make a few comparisons. We call the supreme being God. The Indians, in particular the Sioux, called God *Wakan Tanka*, the Great Spirit. We say God created all. The Sioux gave thanks to the Great Spirit for the sky, the sun, the moon, the grass, and all things that surrounded them on the earth and in the heavens. Pretty close comparisons, wouldn't you say?

Angels can appear in any shape, size, or form, and to anyone at any time, so why couldn't they have appeared to the noble Indian? Perhaps we have a problem with that because these appearances did not take on the conventional form of a being in a white robe, golden halo, and snow-white wings, but rather the Indians saw visions of a great warrior, an eagle, a large white stallion, or a white buffalo—all things to which they could easily relate. Indians put great store in translating the meanings of their dreams and vision. And their faith in such things was not only great, but well-founded.

The following story seems to go so well with the verse that I selected for the beginning of this section. After you have read of this Indian boy's dream, return to the verse and read it again slowly, and see if it does not have the same profound effect on you that it had on me.

# 10

# The Vision

WHEN ONE SPEAKS OF FAMOUS INDIAN CHIEFS, THE FIRST name that generally comes to mind is that of Sitting Bull, chief of the mighty Hunkpapa Sioux nation. This is understandable because Sitting Bull is automatically linked with George Armstrong Custer and the battle of the Little Bighorn, better known as Custer's Last Stand.

What very few people realize is that Sitting Bull himself never fired a single shot or a single arrow in that famed battle on June 25, 1876. During the actual fighting, Sitting Bull sat in his lodge and prayed to the Great Spirit, asking for a great victory for his warriors. The fighting was led by another Sioux chief, a famed warrior named Tashunca-uitco. To us, and to the unfortunate men of Custer's command, he is known as Crazy Horse.

Born around 1840 or 1841 near present-day Rapid City, South Dakota, Crazy Horse was the son of a Oglala Sioux medicine man. His childhood name was

Curly and he was a healthy, strong lad, although a loner. He preferred to stay in the background, watching and listening to all that went on around him. He learned by observing the actions of the mighty chiefs and wise elders. Thought to be strange by others his age, Curly would often go off for days by himself to ponder the things he had heard and observed among the Sioux leaders of his people.

At the age of sixteen, Curly went into the mountains with a hunting party. As they rested that night, the young boy dreamed he was standing on the edge of a cliff on a great mountain, staring up at the clouds in the sky when, suddenly, from out of those clouds came a vision of a great warrior. He was dressed in a white warbonnet, white buffalo shirt, and white moccasins. He rode a great white stallion and carried a white lance with a golden tip.

The sky around the warrior suddenly went dark and threatening. Bolts of lightning, brighter than any the boy had ever witnessed, struck around the warrior and his mighty steed. Small streaks of light flew all about the spirit, narrowly missing him as he rode proud and straight.

The spirit's voice was strong and rumbled like thunder as he spoke. He told Curly that a great warrior would rise from the Sioux nation and become a strong leader of his people. He would lead them in many battles, and through his leadership great victories would come to the Sioux. Although many of those who followed him would fall to his left and right, he would not be harmed by the weapons of his enemies. And when his death came it would not be on the battlefield, but rather in a place of great sadness, and one of his own would take part in that death.

After returning from the hunt, Curly told his father of the vision. The father listened, then proudly called the other elders together and had his son repeat the dream. A great murmuring rose from around the council fire, and all agreed that it was a true vision that foretold of the lad's future greatness as a warrior and leader. From that day, the boy Curly no longer existed. He was given a new name, a warrior's name. And that name would forever be Crazy Horse.

The promise of Crazy Horse's dream was amply realized. He fought alongside the great war chief Red Cloud in the war of the Bozeman Trail and was among those who annihilated Captain William J. Fetterman, a boastful cavalry officer who said that in a party of eighty cavalrymen he could ride through the entire Sioux nation. One day he tried to fulfill his boast. By sunset of that same day, Captain Fetterman and the other seventy-nine men with him were dead. The U.S. government withdrew from further use of the Bozeman Trail.

Following the Sioux victory in the Bozeman conflict, Crazy Horse was made war chief of the Oglala Sioux and also commanded a large following from the Brules and Northern Cheyenne. All had heard the story of Crazy Horse's vision, and at the slaughter of Fedderman's forces they had watched the brave warrior ride headlong into the gunfire of the soldiers time after time, and not one bullet had touched him.

Crazy Horse rose to his greatest prominence during the Sioux War for the Black Hills. To the Sioux, these mountains in present-day South Dakota were regarded as a holy place, the home of *Wakan Tanka,* the Great Spirit. Darkly wooded, therefore "black," and watered by many beautiful rivers and streams, the Black Hills became the physical as well as the

spiritual center of Sioux life, a holy place not to be
spoiled by the whites. (The Federal Government was
well aware of this. In past treaties, the Indians had
relented and allowed whites to move them about and
take their land a little at a time. But the Indians
warned that any attempt to steal the Black Hills from
them would result in a war that would bring together
all the Plains Indians for one last great battle. Washington promised that those hills would always remain
the land of the Sioux. As usual, that promise turned
out to be another lie. Of all the treaties signed between the American government and the American
Indian, not one was ever kept.)

On the seventeenth of June 1876, thirteen hundred
U.S. troopers under the command of General George
Crook attacked a village on the upper Rosebud Creek
in the Black Hills. Crazy Horse quickly organized
his warriors, and with a force of twelve hundred
Sioux and Cheyenne rode out to do battle with the
army. Using tactics that totally baffled General
Crook, Crazy Horse dealt the troopers a terrible blow.
His losses staggering, General Crook quickly withdrew under the pressure of Crazy Horse's relentless
attacks.

In the village that night there was great happiness
and dancing. The Sioux had defeated the soldiers and
won a great victory. Once again Crazy Horse had led
his people in battle, and once again he had defied
the bullets of his enemies. Even though other warriors around him had been knocked from their horses
by the hail of bullets that met their every charge
against the soldiers, Crazy Horse had not sustained
a single scratch.

One week following General Crook's defeat at the
Rosebud, Crazy Horse fought another great battle

against the U.S. Cavalry. The date was June 25, 1876. The flamboyant General George Armstrong Custer, unaware of Crook's defeat on the Rosebud, led the Seventh Cavalry into the Little Bighorn Valley in search of hostile Indians. What he found in that valley far exceeded the number of Indians he expected to encounter. Having split his command earlier, Custer rode to the attack with only 225 men, fully expecting the Indians to panic and scatter as they had done so many times before. But on this day, it was not to be. Fueled by their victory over Crook and led by their fearless war chief Crazy Horse, over four thousand Indians rode out to meet the self-proclaimed great Indian fighter, George Armstrong Custer.

According to the warrior Two-Moons, who rode beside Crazy Horse that day, "The battle took only as long as it would take a hungry man to eat his dinner."

Custer and every man with him was killed in what is still referred to as Custer's Last Stand, without a doubt, the most famous Indian battle of all time. And once again Crazy Horse had emerged from a great battle unharmed.

Following the battle of the Little Bighorn, Crazy Horse led a brilliant campaign against one of the army's best commanders, General Nelson A. Miles. But the never-ending wave of soldiers relentlessly pursued the Indians across the country. Winter set in and food was scarce. Miles knew that if he could keep the pressure on, the Indians would eventually have to give up and return to the reservations. And so it was that Crazy Horse, seeing the great suffering of his people, surrendered on May 5, 1877.

As part of his surrender terms, Crazy Horse was

promised a reservation for the Ogala Sioux on the Powder River. But that was a lie, as had been all promises made by the whites. Crazy Horse and his people were to remain on the Red Cloud reservation forever.

Government officials began to worry about the power of Crazy Horse. He was still considered a great warrior and Sioux leader among the young warriors. General Crook received word from the reservation agent that Crazy Horse was "an incorrigible wild man, silent, sullen, lordly, and dictatorial," and the agent feared the war chief was fomenting an uprising among the young men. General Crook responded by having Crazy Horse arrested and moved to Camp Robinson, in the northwest corner of Nebraska.

As he was being led to his new cell at Camp Robinson, Crazy Horse saw a number of his people being held in cattle pens. Their suffering shone in their eyes and their weather-beaten faces, and it pained him to look upon them. For the Sioux, this was truly a place of great sadness.

Among the soldiers escorting Crazy Horse to his cell were a number of government Indian police. Whether one of these men said something to Crazy Horse is not known, but for some unexplained reason a scuffle broke out in front of the war chief's cell. In the ensuing fight, Crazy Horse broke free and ran a few yards before being grabbed by a Sioux policeman who pinned his arms while a soldier stabbed him in the side with a bayonet.

Crazy Horse knelt down holding his side and began singing his death song. His imprisoned people held their hands up to the Great Spirit. Tears flowed down their faces as they watched the dying of a great war chief, who, as a boy, had received a true vision from the Great Spirit in a holy place known as the Black Hills.

As Crazy Horse drew his last breath, he was surrounded by his people in a place of great sadness. The prophecy of the Great Spirit warrior had been fulfilled.

## 11

# *Sanko, the Kiowa Believer*

FOLLOWING THE INDIAN WARS, THE KIOWAS FOUND themselves on a reservation near present-day Fort Sill, Oklahoma. The time of great battles in the hope of recovering all they had lost was gone for the American Indian. They had fought hard, but stopping the westward expansion of the whites had proven hopeless. There were just too many of them. For each one they eliminated, five took his place. Resigned to their fate, the Kiowas took up the way of the reservation Indian.

The following story is about a battle between two Indians, both Kiowa. It was a battle between two faiths and between good and evil. In late 1895 Baptist missionaries built a small mission in the Rainy Mountain area of the Kiowa reservation. The mission was operated by two women, Miss Reeside and Miss Ballew. Their interpreter and assistant was a full-blood Kiowa girl named Julia Given, the daughter of the late chief Santank. The three lived in a small cottage near the mission and went about their work of teaching the word of God and Christianity to all the Kiowas who wished to learn.

One of those who strongly resented their presence and rejected their religion was Tone-a-koy, a powerful Kiowa medicine man who was said to possess the power of evil and was reputed to have used that power on a number of occasions to strike dead those who offended him. Tone-a-koy had taken up the peyote cult religion and had been steadily building a large group of followers from around the surrounding area. He saw the white missionaries and their Christianity as a threat and constantly spoke ill of their God and their religion to maintain control over his followers.

However, one of the younger members of the peyote circle, a young Kiowa named Sanko, had secretly gone to the mission with the daughter of a friend to hear the words of the white missionaries. The fact that the daughter of the great chief Santank had herself embraced the religion of the missionaries further evoked his interest in the teachings of the white women.

Before long, Sanko converted to Christianity. Normally a conversion would not have caused a problem, for even Tone-a-koy realized that he could not stop everyone from visiting the mission and that it was inevitable that some would take up the whites' religion. But when Tone-a-koy heard of Sanko's conversion he went into a rage. The boy had been one of his assistants and understudies in the peyote cult. To allow one of his own apprentices to desert him for the whites' religion could open the gates for more to follow. Tone-a-koy had to do something to show his power and make the boy return to him and the cult.

Several times Sanko was warned to abandon the white religion and return to the old ways, and to do it at once, but each time he was warned, the young Kiowa refused to abandon his newfound God. Rumors began to pass among the Indians far and wide that unless this foolish boy did as Tone-a-koy demanded, the medicine man would call forth his evil powers and set them upon the boy, and when that day came the boy was sure to die.

One afternoon the Kiowas at Rainy Mountain Creek were butchering a steer for a feast at the camp of Big Tree, a Kiowa chief. Sanko was there enjoying himself when Tone-a-koy rode up. Big Tree invited the medicine man to join them.

Tone-a-koy, anger clear in his face, rudely refused, then directed his glare toward the Christian convert: "Sanko, I am going to warn you for the last time. Give up the white man's god! Walk away from the white god's teaching and quit this mission business entirely. Return to the Indian way. Do you get my meaning from my words?"

Sanko replied, steadily, "I have taken the Jesus road, Tone-a-koy. When I take up a new road, I keep it."

The medicine man's scowl deepened. "You are doing a very dangerous thing. This Jesus is only the white man's god. He is not for the Indian. I am telling you, you had better give up this foolishness!"

Sanko stood tall as he replied, "Tone-a-koy, I have looked all through the old Kiowa religion. I have listened to Pau-tape-ty, who promised to bring back the buffalo. I threw away the lying words of Eadletau-hain, who was going to call down the sun to destroy all the white men. I have danced the Ghost Dance until my feet have bled, and watched it fade away. I have even been a faithful worshipper at the peyote altar, but there is nothing in any of these medicines.

"But the Jesus road is kindness. It says to love your brothers, which we Indians have always known was good. The white god is the Great Spirit. He loves us all. I believe in His words of promise and in His strong medicine. I have taken it close to my heart, and I will hold it fast."

"Give it up!" growled Tone-a-koy.

"I cannot," Sanko insisted.

The other Indians had broken off their conversation and were listening intently.

"Do you want to live a long life, Sanko?" asked the medicine man.

Sanko wet his lips, "I do. But I am not afraid to die. I am not afraid of your medicine."

"Then in that case," said Tone-a-koy furiously, "you had better dig your grave. You are not going to live more than two days. I'll see to that."

Though badly frightened, Sanko stood his ground. "I will not follow your gods," he said. "They offer no salvation." Taking a step toward the medicine man, Sanko looked up at him, and with confidence in his voice said, "It is you who should be warned, Tone-a-koy. Those who willingly walk the Jesus road do not do so alone. They are guarded from evil by the Father's army of warriors who serve Him. I am not afraid of you. They will protect me against your evil power."

Tone-a-koy leaned back on his horse, a slight smirk on his face. Shifting his gaze over the other men present, he said, "Tomorrow my women will build my medicine lodge at the foot of Rainy Mountain. After sundown I will work my power. I will dispose of Sanko. I want all the people to see it, so they will know whose god is the strongest. Announce it through all the camps. I want all Kiowas to be there." Turning his eyes back on the Indian boy, he continued, "In the meantime, this poor little Sanko had better get busy and pray to his newfound god."

Sanko went home. He had stood up to the medicine man but was truly frightened. That night he could not sleep. By morning he was physically shaking. He got up, saddled his horse, and rode to the missionary cabin. Miss Reeside met him at the door.

"Why, Sanko!" she cried. "What is wrong? You look sick."

"I have big trouble," he said brokenly. "Want help."

"Come in and tell us about it," said the missionary, opening the door wide for him.

Sanko sat at a table and told the whole story of what had happened. When the women tried to reassure him that all would be fine, not to worry, Sanko insisted that the medicine man had succeeded in doing harm to his enemies before. He cited a long list of cases known to the entire tribe, in which Tone-a-koy had used his power for evil.

"What shall I do, so that my God's power will stand against that of Tone-a-koy's god?" he asked.

The women were still inclined to make light of the problem. They assured Sanko that superstition could not harm him, that a Christian was above such things.

Julia Given quickly took up for Sanko. "You do not understand these things, Miss Reeside. You cannot break the power of the witch doctor simply by saying that his powers do not exist. To the Indian they are very real. I have seen some of these things myself, and they are truly hard to explain."

"Then we must pray," said the women. "God will help us."

They all knelt down and prayed for a long time. Their prayers were earnest and sincere. They asked for divine help for Sanko in his time of trial. When they were finished, tears were running down their cheeks—including Sanko's.

For a time Sanko felt better. He returned home and fell upon his bed and tried to make up some of the sleep he had lost the night before. But his eyes wouldn't close. He could not banish the anxiety that was now returning. He felt as though his very heart were being gripped by a pair of icy hands.

Tone-a-koy, having slept soundly through the night, waited until midafternoon to direct his women to put up his medicine lodge at the base of Rainy Mountain. Working under his supervision, they also laid a bonfire near the tepee entrance and erected a smaller tepee at the rear, which he would use as a dressing room and a place for his props for the performance.

Late in the day Tone-a-koy went to the medicine lodge and, with the flaps closed, prepared the scenery for the big act. Then he went into the smaller tepee, where he devoted an hour to painting himself and donning his costume.

By this time the sun had set and the people were beginning to arrive and gather in a semicircle, seated on the ground some twenty to thirty paces from the door of the main tepee. Few people spoke, and those who did, did so in whispers. They were all filled with superstitious fear, but could not stay away. Even Sanko, the intended victim, came at the last moment

and hovered at the edge of the crowd, no one noticing him in the gathering darkness.

Finally Tone-a-koy's wives lit the fire, which illu-
minated the tepee with a wavering light. They stood
on either side of the door and at a given signal from
within pulled back the flaps, exposing the interior
to view.

A great murmur arose from those in the semicircle,
followed by a long-drawn expression of amazement
and wonder as they stared inside. On the ground on
one side of the lodge was a fire hole filled with glowing embers. On the other side was a miniature lake
or pond, realistically constructed with moss in the
center and willow twigs around the edges to represent
trees, and filled with water. Between the pond and
the fire hole was the effigy of a man lying on his
back with his arms outstretched. The figure was fash-
ioned from earth, and in the chest, over the heart,
was a heart-shaped hole about six inches deep. Every
person there knew who was represented by that
figure.

Suddenly the booming of a bullfrog was heard,
first low, then growing louder. Through a slit in the
rear wall of the tepee a grotesque figure entered,
leaped to the front, and stood full in the light of the
fire. It was a giant frog. Tone-a-koy had very cleverly
painted his entire body with yellow splotches. Over
his head he had slipped a realistic mask made of
leather and painted to represent the head of a frog,
with its bulbous eyes and wide, gaping mouth. As
Tone-a-koy vowed that his great powers came from
the underwater world, it was appropriate that his costume represented one of the lake creatures. No doubt
the adults present knew full well that this was the
medicine man. But the children did not, and even a

few of the elders were frightened by the sight. There were some choked-off cries of fear and a good deal of whimpering.

Never had the Kiowas seen anything so fearsome.

After a short pause to allow the full effect of his appearance to take hold, the medicine man began his dance. He squatted, he leaped, he waddled like a frog. Then he began to gyrate, shaking his rattle and chanting his special, sinister songs.

Now and then he pointed to various objects in the lodge, while in his chant he explained which medicine they represented and boasted of the power that they gave him. He was doing very well indeed, and the effect on the crowd and especially on the hapless Sanko, was all that he could have wished for.

At length he stopped, took up a metal dipper, and scooped up some live coals from the fire hole. With a flourish and a wicked grin he poured these into the heart of the effigy. At that moment Sanko felt an agonizing pain in his chest. Cold sweat stood out all over him.

Now Tone-a-koy began the dreaded death prayer. With his arms outstretched and upward and the leather flaps that he had fastened to his hands and feet in imitation of the web feet of the frog beating a tattoo, he prayed to the south, west, north, and east in turn. The prayers were loud, clear, and completely understandable. They called on the underwater devils to strike Sanko dead at a certain signal that he was about to give. As he alternately drew near the bonfire, then away, Tone-a-koy's shadow on the back of the tepee looked like a misshapen dwarf, then blew up to that of a monster, its claws outstretched menacingly.

Sanko was choking, his knees buckling.

The crowd was transfixed. Every man, woman, and child was holding his breath.

Quickly the tempo of the dance increased. The weird chant rose to a screech. At the climax, Tone-a-koy seized a loaded rifle, pointed it at the heart of the effigy, and fired.

Sanko saw no more. He had fallen to the ground, unconscious.

But what the crowd witnessed that night has never been explained. To many it was a miracle. As the reverberations of the rifle shot faded, a second figure, dressed in all white, appeared to materialize out of the gunsmoke. The figure's hand rose and passed once from left to right in front of Tone-a-koy, then disappeared once more into the smoke that drifted out of the flap of the tepee and up into the night sky.

The final whiffs of smoke had no sooner cleared the tepee than the medicine man suddenly clutched wildly at his midsection. He tore off his hideous mask, disclosing an agonized expression. Tone-a-koy swayed for a moment, then fell heavily on his face.

Before anyone could move, his two wives rushed in and turned him over. Foam appeared on his blue lips. His breathing was labored. The gasps came more and more slowly. Then they stopped altogether. Tone-a-koy was dead.

The people were on their feet now, stunned and speechless at what they had witnessed. As they stared at the body of the vanquished shaman, Tone-a-koy's wives began to wail over the death of their husband. They were soon joined by the medicine man's sister, who ran forward and fell to cry at her brother's side. Knives appeared. The mourners began to gash themselves—on their arms, breasts, and faces. The blood flowed over their garments as a sign of their grief.

The wailing became louder. Miss Reeside and Miss Ballew, who had refrained from attending the gathering, though they knew what was taking place, heard the crying. They crossed the creek to comfort Tone-a-koy's women. Soon their dresses too were covered in blood.

Someone, discovering Sanko passed out on the ground, threw water on his face to revive him. He sat up, blinked his eyes, and rose unsteadily to his feet. He was filled with wonder. He was alive, not a spirit! Gradually he realized that the wailing was not for him, but for his enemy, who was lying dead in the light of the fire.

Sanko pushed through the crowd as he made his way to the side of the mourning wives. He looked down at Tone-a-koy. Then he faced his people. His eyes were shining. He raised his arms to the heavens and shouted for all to hear, "My God win! My God win!"

# WORLD WAR I

WORLD WAR I RANKS SECOND ONLY TO WORLD WAR II as the bloodiest and costliest war in modern history. The monetary cost was more than $337 billion. The cost in military lives was more than 8 million killed.

Three pistol shots signaled the start of the war. An armistice ended the fighting four long years later.

(Readers may recognize some of the names of the places where this war began. If you do not, then you have only to watch the nightly news or read today's newspaper.)

Shortly before noon on Sunday, June 28, 1914, crowds gathered in Sarajevo, the capital of the Austrian province of Bosnia. They had come to see Archduke Francis Ferdinand, heir to the throne of Austria-Hungary, and his wife, Sophie.

As the archduke and his wife rode through the streets of Sarajevo, a man suddenly jumped onto the running board of the royal touring car and fired a pistol. Two shots struck the archduke and one hit his wife, who was trying to shield him from the assassin. They both died almost instantly. The three shots fired that day were the spark that ignited a world war and hurtled the world into the modern age. They signaled a loss of innocence that cannot be recaptured.

World War I was unlike any other war the world had fought up to that time. New and improved weapons gave both sides more efficient machines with which to kill each other. Mechanized vehicles—tanks, trucks, automobiles, and motorcycles—speeded the war on land, while, for the first time, airplanes and airships fought in the skies and bombed soldiers and civilians. On the sea, submarines torpedoed merchant ships without warning.

Perhaps, to the men who fought this war, fear of new weaponry was nothing compared to the misery of a new type of fighting—trench warfare. Fighting on the western front reached a standstill in early 1915, and the deadlock continued for almost two years. Both sides dug in and built networks of trenches that stretched for over six hundred miles across France and Belgium. In some places less than one hundred yards separated the opposing lines.

Between these lines of trenches lay "no-man's-land."

"Over the top!" a battlefront commander would yell. Infantrymen with fixed bayonets clamored out of their trenches and dashed across no-man's-land. They tossed their grenades, struggled through barbed-wire entanglements, and ran around gaping shell holes—under almost constant machine-gun fire. Losses were staggering and, more often than not, made successful charges impossible.

As time went on, more trenches were dug forming

a second and third line so that troops and supplies could be moved to and from the front. Huge underground caverns served as aid stations, supply centers, and living quarters. The troops found life in the trenches miserable even when they were not fighting. Rain filled the dugouts with water and mud, and rats swarmed through the trenches. During lulls in the fighting, battle communiques reported: "All quiet on the western front."

It was a new age, with new weapons and new enemies. (I often find myself thinking, "The more things change, the more they remain the same.")

Although the men, the uniforms, and the weapons had changed for this war, one thing that had not changed was men's belief in their religion. No matter how alone or lost they might feel, there was always someone to whom they could turn in time of need.

The following are a few of the stories from this war that was supposed to have been "the war to end all wars."

## 12

# The Legend of Albert

DURING THE BATTLE OF SOMME, IN FRANCE, A LEGEND was born: the legend of Albert Cathedral.

Albert was an old industrial city that stood on the Ancre overlooking a refreshing waterfall. Throughout the carnage of the battle for the Somme, the city of Albert was shelled severely almost on a daily basis. During one such bombardment the painted statue of the Virgin that graced the tower of the church of Notre-Dame—Brebieris was nearly destroyed.

A shell struck the upper portion of the tower, and the steel supports that carried the weight of the figure, instead of giving way, were bent so that the Virgin, still holding the Christ Child in her outstretched arms, hung precariously over the rubble in the street.

Over the months, those passing through the shattered but still standing town would stop and stare in understandable awe at the dangling figure of the Virgin Mary and Christ Child hanging haphazardly out over the street. There were all sorts of suggestions and speculation about what modern miracle held the holy statue in place.

As a number of the former residents of Albert returned to poke about the ruins of what had once been their quiet homes, a group of flyers on pass could not resist asking one elderly resident what he thought of the precarious position of the Virgin.

Removing his hat respectfully, he gazed up at the sacred statue and with great enthusiasm stated, "That is a token from our God. Our Blessed Virgin is held firmly by His angels as a sign of hope to us. You wait and see. One day the angels will release her and she will come down, and when that happens, the war will end."

The pilots looked at one another, thanked the elderly man for his observations, and went on their way. Once they were out of sight of the old man, one snickered and asked, "Did you ever hear such blarney in your life?"

No one laughed. To some, it might be just the ramblings of an old man who had lost everything, but to each of them the story held a glimmer of hope and evidence of something clean and sacred amid the ruins and death that surrounded them. It was a story that would cross the minds of these flyers often throughout the war.

And rightly so. For on November 10, 1918, a stray German shell struck Albert Cathedral again—and the Virgin came tumbling down.

The next day, November 11, 1918, the Germans signed the Armistice. World War I was over.

## 13

# A Battle Prayer

ALTHOUGH THIS SHORT SECTION OF MY BOOK DOES NOT contain a miraculous sighting, vision, or occurrence, I found the following poem among the mounds of research materials stacked around my computer one day and could not resist including it.

For those of you who have never experienced war and the terror that it creates in both its survivors and its victims, I offer this prayer. It is only one of countless thousands that have been written by men in battle, in every war. The times may change. The places, the faces, the names—they too change, but a soldier's courage will forever be anchored by his belief that he is not alone. Should he fall in battle, the angels will escort his soul to that higher place where he shall know peace.

This is a poem written by William H. Harrah, a private in the 23rd Infantry of the American Expeditionary Force. Private Harrah celebrated his twentieth birthday in June 1918. At the time his unit was involved in the bitter battle at Belleau Wood in France. It is believed that this poem was written at some point during that battle.

Private Harrah was reported missing in action near Vierzy, France, on July 19, 1918. Out of honor and respect to this young man, I include his words in this book.

## A Battle Prayer

*Alone upon a hill I stand*
*And look o'er the trenches in no-man's land.*
*In night's black skies, like northern lights,*
*The pale flashes rise.*
*To mark the dark heights where death's angels*
  *bear away*
*The souls of men who died today....*

*Out there lie men who died for right,*
*Oh, Christ, be merciful tonight.*
*Wilt the one who stilled the troubled sea*
*Stretch forth Thy hand their pain to ease,*
*Thy sons whose feet trod earth's battlefield,*
*Oh, Son of God.*

## 14

# The Avenging Angel of Neuve-Chapelle

THE EVENTS OF THIS STORY TOOK PLACE DURING THE battle of Neuve-Chapelle, a small village in Belgium, in March 1915. The Germans had turned the once peaceful, serene village into a virtual fortress. Every house had been reinforced to establish strongholds throughout the town. Outside the town, a number of villas had been strengthened and interconnected with former French fortifications that linked fields and orchards. It was a mighty complex supported by scattered machine gun positions throughout. Taking the small village of Neuve-Chapelle was going to be very costly no matter how well planned the strategy.

The task fell to the British IV Corps under General Sir Henry Rawlinson, and the Indian Corps, crack Gurkha troops from India, under General Sir James Willcocks.

On the night of March 9, General Willcocks summoned one of the Indian sergeants and four of his best Indian troopers. They were to move through the British lines and infiltrate the village of Neuve-Chapelle. Once there, they would recon the defenses and attempt to find a weak point that could be exploited by the regiment once a planned artillery barrage was lifted.

As the sergeant and his men prepared for their mission, a British corporal approached the leader. Knowing the hazards of his comrades' mission, he had written the Lord's Prayer on the back of a piece of cardboard box. He gave it to the sergeant. The Indian leader thanked the corporal for the gesture and for his concern, but told him that should he die an honorable death, then it was merely his time to depart this earthly evil.

"But what if the Germans should capture you?" asked the worried soldier.

Such concern was indeed justified. The Germans considered the Indian troops, with their dark skins, no more than savages, and therefore did not recognize them as soldiers entitled to the protection due military men in combat, but rather as animals to be slaughtered. The Indian troops clearly understood that should they fall into enemy hands, no quarter or mercy would be given.

The Indian sergeant again assured the corporal that all would be fine, not to worry. He was a Hindu. His religion believed in reincarnation. Should less than an honorable death befall him, his spirit would return in the form of God's avenging angel and wreak a terrible havoc upon his slayers.

Pressing the prayer into the sergeant's hand, the corporal said no more and returned to his position on the line. As dusk fell over the battlefield, the corporal watched the five brave men go over the top of the trench and disappear into the ground fog of no-man's-land. They did not return.

The following morning, the corporal was awakened by a sorrowful cry and the cursing of his comrades in the trench. Jumping to his feet and peering over the trench line, he saw the five Indian soldiers stripped and spread-eagled across the front of the enemy barbed wire. Their flesh had been sliced in strips and their heads cut off and planted on spikes next to their bodies. It was indeed a sickening sight.

Outraged, the men in the trenches cursed under their breath and swore vengeance. But as early morning passed into afternoon, their rage slowly turned to depression. The corporal especially was despondent. He wondered what had happened to his prayer written on the cardboard box. Had the sergeant repeated it before the end came?

After finding a piece of paper, he began to write the verse again. Midway through his writing, he felt the presence of someone standing over him. When he looked up, he found himself staring at another Gurkha sergeant. In his belt, the man carried the famous Gurkha knife, a great curved blade that was a variant of the Malay kris. One of the unwritten rules concerning these famous knives was that they could never be drawn from their scabbards without being bloodied before being returned to their proper place. But this blade was not like others any of the men in the trench had seen—this one was made of pure silver with jewels encased in the handle. It was the most beautiful thing any of them had ever seen.

The Gurkha sergeant was tall and lean, his eyes coal-black and piercing. His very presence sent a chill down the spines of many of those around him. Looking up at the man, the corporal asked, "May I help you, Sergeant?"

Although neither the corporal nor any of the men in the trench had ever met this man before, he answered softly, "You already have." He then turned and walked to the far end of the trench, where he stood alone, gazing out over the battlefield in silence. All anyone knew was that he was apparently a late-arriving replacement assigned to their unit, but no one knew his name.

That night British intelligence requested that another Gurkha patrol be sent out to dispatch a few of the enemy. Once this was done, they were to cut off the shoulder epaulets from the dead men's uniforms, then return to British lines. By studying the insignia, Intelligence could identify what enemy regiments or divisions they were up against.

Although not selected for the mission, the mysterious new arrival, who had spoken only those three words to the corporal, moved to the front of the ready-ladders at the base of the trench and prepared to go over the top with the other Gurkhas. Seeing this, a British officer moved toward the man to protest, but the Gurkha with the silver blade stopped him with only a cold stare. The officer backed away from the ladder without uttering a word. Within seconds the patrol was up and over, slowly making their way toward the enemy lines. Those remaining in the trenches stared out into the darkness of the pock-marked terrain, silently praying for their comrades moving quietly from crater to crater.

As shells exploded overhead, a rash of whispers spread quickly along the line as glimmers of light flashed off the blade of the silver Gurkha knife that had clearly been unsheathed in the middle of no-man's-land.

Once the Indian patrol broke into the enemy trenches, the owner of the silver blade set about his work with a vengeance as, with perfect precision, he moved along each enemy position and with a professional swipe, unmatched by any ever witnessed by his fellow Gurkhas, he practically sliced off the head of every unfortunate he encountered. Two Germans stood and fired point-blank at the tall sergeant. At that range it seemed impossible for them to have missed the giant of a man, but nevertheless, he continued to swing the flashing blade, dispatching them both.

Within minutes the Gurkha leader of the patrol had more than enough epaulets. The mission had been completed and he began to blow his whistle for the recall signal. Scrambling back to their leader, the other Gurkhas began to yell to their new member to rejoin them, but the Gurkha with the silver knife ignored their calls and continued on through the enemy trenches, his blade moving with lightning speed and deadly accuracy. Soon he was lost in the darkness, amid the shooting and screams of the German trench.

That was the last anyone ever saw of the Gurkha with the silver knife, but not the last that was heard of him. For weeks after that raid, the German high command complained that a whole tribe of Indian savages was at large hacking off the heads of unsuspecting German soldiers. An official complaint was filed with an international court at the Hague, but no one ever found the strangely silent but deadly effective and mysterious Gurkha, or his dazzling silver blade.

Following the war, a search of records for that

area and time showed no Gurkha replacements ever being sent to Neuve-Chapelle. Who was this man without a name who had appeared from nowhere? He had spoken only three words, and those to one man, the corporal who had written a prayer on a piece of cardboard.

"You already have." What did this stranger mean by those three words? Why the uncommon kris of silver? Never was another like it seen through the war. How could two combat-hardened enemy soldiers fire a series of shots at a man point-blank, and miss? Did they really miss their mark?

Could this have been an avenging angel as prophesied by the murdered sergeant only the night before?

These are questions that were asked years later by the British corporal and all who came into contact with the mysterious Gurkha that day at Neuve-Chapelle. Had they unknowingly looked upon the face of an avenging angel?

# 15

# *The Angel of Mons*

> *Be not forgetful to entertain strangers: for thereby some have entertained angels unawares.*

> —HEBREWS 13:2

AT THE OUTBREAK OF WORLD WAR I GREAT BRITAIN'S Lord Horatio H. Kitchener asked for a half-million volunteers to fight against the German war machine. The volunteers would be fighting for God, queen, and country. The response was so overwhelming that many of the volunteers had to be sent home to await openings and the manufacture of uniforms and the required combat gear.

Among Britain's many heroic and colorful units was the Coldstream Guard, better known as the Coldstreamers. A proud and historic unit, they were first organized by Oliver Cromwell in 1650. From the point of age, they are the senior guards regiment of the British army. These men were first-class regulars, highly trained, and, more importantly, inspired by regimental tradition.

On August 23, 1914, members of the British Expeditionary Force faced their first true test of battle in the great war to end all wars. It came at a place called Mons, the capital of Hainaut Province in Belgium.

The BEF had crossed the channel and landed at Le Havre, under the protection of the Royal Navy. They were deployed along a line behind the Mons-Conde Canal, which offered them some protection from German artillery. As the Germans pressed their attacks, the French, Britain's ally on the right flank, began to suffer heavy casualties. Shortly thereafter, the French defenses began to crumble under the German onslaught. They had no alternative but to withdraw, leaving the British right flank unprotected and wide open to attack. Seeing this, the Germans were quick to take advantage of the situation and pressed their attack, swinging the German First Army headlong at the weakened flank of the British Expeditionary Force. It would prove to be a disastrous mistake.

British pride, guts, and superb rifle fire immediately took a deadly toll of the German attack force. The assault was shattered by the withering fire and broke, sending the survivors scurrying back to their own lines and the safety of the German trenches.

Once safely inside their own lines, German commanders of the attack force frantically called their higher command headquarters to explain their sudden retreat. They quickly explained that their German forces had been outnumbered ten to one by the British. On this point the German commanders of the First Army were somewhat incorrect. The odds *had* been ten to one, but it was the British who were

outnumbered, not the Germans. The unit that had
formed the nucleus of the British stand that day had
been the Coldstream Guard.

For the British, however, this was a short-lived
victory. As night descended over the battlefield, the
Germans began a link-up maneuver in an effort to
encircle the British force. Allied commanders, still
reeling from the loss of the French positions, could
not send reinforcements, and therefore ordered an immediate withdrawal of the British force. As expected,
the Coldstream Guard would cover the retreat and
would be the last unit out of the area.

A few hours before morning, the Coldstreamers
were notified that all Allied units had escaped the
rapidly closing German circle and were themselves
ordered to withdraw as quickly as possible. In the
half-light of a false dawn the lead element of the
Coldstreamers became disoriented and wandered
about in the semidarkness in an attempt to make contact with their main body. When it became painfully
obvious that they were completely out of touch with
any Allied forces, the Coldstreamers began to dig in,
determined to make another heroic stand at dawn.

In the still darkness they could hear the rattling
equipment of the enemy as they brought up reinforcements and began to close the circle more tightly
around the Coldstreamers. The men of the
Coldstream Guard continued to improve their positions. Their spirits were high, even though they all
knew full well that with the coming sunrise, these
very same holes that they had dug in the earth could
well become their own graves.

One of the younger members of the guard spoke
with a tone of hope, saying that possibly Allied aid
could reach them by dawn, but that idea was quickly

dashed by the regimental color sergeant. No one knew where they were. There was no need to build false hopes.

At that moment another guardsman looked up from his digging and noticed a warm glow just beyond their position. For a second he thought someone was wandering about with a lantern. He quickly alerted the others. Everyone stopped digging and watched the light. Someone said it could be a farmer searching for his lost barnyard stock. Another joked that it was possibly a ghost. "No matter what it is," said the color sergeant, "wandering about a battlefield with a lantern is bloody suicide."

As the light drew closer, the guardsmen began to see the dim outline of a female figure. As it came closer, it became more distinct. Every last man of the guard stood stock-still and stared in awe at the sight. "My word!" gasped the veteran color sergeant, rubbing his eyes, then staring again at the approaching light.

The figure looked remarkably like one of the many representations of angels they had seen numerous times in the regimental chapel: tall, slim, and wearing a flowing white gown. She had a gold band around her hair and sandals on her feet. A pair of white wings were folded against her slim back.

"She's beckoning to us," muttered one of the guardsmen. There was no doubt about it, the angel was holding out her arm and with a motion of her hand was beckoning them to follow her. Not one member of the guard moved. She drew closer and her signal became more insistent. Anxious looks were exchanged among the Coldstreamers. What were they going to do?

No one remembers who crawled out of their shal-

low battle position first, but one by one the Coldstreamers hauled out their weapons and equipment,
lined up, and followed the glowing figure across an
open field. Not a word was spoken by anyone.

The angel moved on, her right hand still inviting
them to follow until she came to a halt on the upper
rim of a sunken road. The guardsmen were aston-
ished. Earlier they had sent out patrols in all directions to locate a road or path exactly like the one on
which they were now standing, but the patrols had
reported finding nothing, not even a cow path.

The color sergeant registered a blistering stare at
a young guardsman whose patrol had been assigned
to cover this very area earlier. The man was quick
to defend himself, stating flatly that no such road had
existed in the area only a few hours ago. True, one
man could have possibly missed finding the road, but
not all ten men of the patrol. The others agreed.

Raising her hand again, the vision led the way
until all the soldiers had reached the end of the
sunken road, then she floated up the bank and pointed
to a thicket of small trees only a short distance away.
She turned, faced the men of the Coldstream Guard,
smiled a warm, pleasant smile at the amazed men—
then vanished before their very eyes.

Not questioning this strange visitation, the soldiers
made their way to the thicket. Once there, they encountered two British sentries of a regimental forward observation post. They had found their main
force. The sentries were equally excited to see the
Coldstreamers. Headquarters had already written
them off as destroyed in action, or, at the very least,
as prisoners of the Germans.

When the story of the angel of Mons reached the
high command, they pored over every available map

and questioned numerous local residents in an attempt to locate the sunken road identified in the Coldstreamers' highly unusual report, but no such road could be found on any map, nor had any resident ever seen or heard of such a road in that area.

The Coldstreamers, realizing that their honor was now in question, returned to the same area a few days later. In an effort to prove the existence of the road, they scrupulously searched the entire area. Starting at the site of the positions they had dug only a few nights before, the guardsmen fanned out in a search that covered nearly a mile in all directions. No road was ever found.

Today, as then, no one can explain how the Coldstream Guard escaped certain annihilation that night at Mons, but they did. Some members of the present-day regiment often scoff at the legend of the Angel of Mons and argue that these were tired, battle-weary men whose minds were easily fooled by hallucinations. But yet these same guardsmen, only a few days later, went from Mons to an exposed position in another battle area and held their ground, unrelieved, against a vastly superior number of Germans for three weeks—hardly the actions of men suffering from hallucinations.

To this day, no one can positively explain what happened that night to the Coldstream Guard. Nor has anyone ever found the sunken road that provided a path for an angel, and gave life to those whom she protected that night.

# WORLD WAR II

WORLD WAR II KILLED MORE PEOPLE, COST MORE money, damaged more property, and caused more far-reaching changes than any other war in history. It opened the atomic age and brought sweeping changes in the art of warfare. Modern modes of transportation sped infantrymen to the battlefronts after aerial bombing, giant tanks, and pinpoint artillery had "softened" the enemy. Bombers and ballistic missiles rained death and destruction on soldiers, sailors, and civilians alike. Airplanes, warships, and ground forces worked together with split-second timing in amphibious attacks. Paratroopers dropped from airplanes or landed in gliders. The art of war had truly advanced to a higher plane.

The following are but a few of the stories from that war. I am certain many more are out there to be told.

## 16

# An Angel's Wind

In April 1945, the 350th Infantry of the 88th "Blue Devil" Infantry Division was moving through Italy. The American and British advances throughout Europe were closing in on Hitler and Germany's war machine. Many, like Colonel James C. Fry, regimental commander of the 350th Infantry, realized that Hitler's quest for world power was in irreversible decline. It was now only a matter of time.

During the heavy fighting in the northern foothills of the Apennines in Italy, Colonel Fry's unit was in pursuit of a Nazi division that had been driven out of the hills and into the Po Valley. The fighting was bitter and violent across a broad front as the German rear guard made last-ditch stands in an effort to provide their comrades the much-needed time to evacuate as much of their forces and equipment as possible. It was a desperate effort by the Wehrmacht to break contact with Colonel Fry's lead elements and escape the American advance.

As Fry's advance gained momentum, the enemy withdrawal turned into a rout, totally disrupting German communications. With command structure lost, the Nazi forces began to separate into small units with no plans or particular idea of what they were going to do.

Time after time Fry's men encountered small groups of the enemy hiding in barns, ditches, or houses, waiting for darkness and the opportunity to continue their escape northward toward heavily defended German lines.

Most of these groups, when located by the Americans, accepted their fate and surrendered. Others preferred to fight and die. By nightfall, Colonel Fry's troops had secured a large portion of their objective, although the exact location of true battle lines were uncertain.

The following morning, April 18, 1945, Colonel Fry, along with his small staff, moved about the battle area in two jeeps, proceeding to various areas where the commander's presence was needed. It was a beautiful, sunny day, and near noon they stopped and ate lunch under the shade of a barn while the colonel spoke with regimental headquarters on the radio. The situation reports were most optimistic. Large groups of Germans were surrendering and being sent to the rear. No serious fighting was reported anywhere.

Highly pleased with this information, Colonel Fry and his staff continued along their route. Unknowingly, they had passed directly between the two leading American elements and were now in front of their own riflemen and in territory that had not yet been cleared of enemy troops.

As they rounded a bend in the road, Colonel Fry's

aide, Captain Kenneth Brown, spotted a group of men milling around a large stone farmhouse about a hundred yards away. Shielding his eyes from the noonday sun, he suddenly realized what he was looking at. "My God, Colonel! Those are Germans!"

A second later, the jeeps skidded to a halt. The colonel and his men scrambled into a ditch that paralleled the road. There they were temporarily hidden from the enemy by tall grass that grew alongside the ditch.

Cautiously, Colonel Fry parted the grass to observe the German actions. For a moment he gave a sigh of relief. Perhaps they had not been spotted by the Germans. The farmhouse was about a hundred yards away. There was a slight bend in the road that led up to the house, and a small field between the Americans and the Germans. The field had a number of short trees, uncut grass, and high weeds that provided a partial screen for the two jeeps that remained in the middle of the road.

The Americans realized they had stumbled onto a detachment of German infantry that were making their way to the rear. The farmhouse had more than likely been no more than a rest stop for the retreating unit.

Captain Brown knelt down beside the colonel and asked if they had been seen. The colonel replied that he did not think so. The Germans obviously had wounded with them, judging by the number of litters he saw on the ground. After a few minutes, some of the Germans reached down and began to pick up the litters and started moving out toward the German lines. There were, however, still three rifle squads standing around in the front yard.

For Colonel Fry and his men the next few minutes

seemed like an eternity. If it came to a showdown, they were sure to lose the battle. There were only six Americans, and their armament consisted of only three pistols, two rifles, and a limited amount of ammunition. Not a very formidable force to go up against thirty well-armed, combat-hardened German troops.

Time inched by slowly, and for a moment it seemed as if they had escaped certain disaster. Ten of the Germans slung their rifles and walked off in the direction of the litter bearers. Perhaps the others would be moving soon, thought Fry. They did . . . but the wrong way.

Suddenly the twenty remaining Germans fanned out and began running across the field straight for the area in which the Americans were hiding with the obvious intention of killing them once they had been accurately located.

Captain Brown pulled his .45 automatic pistol and muttered, "My God, Colonel, this is it."

As if he were drowning, a thousand things ran through the colonel's mind. What should he do? Should he try to surrender his small group? Would the Germans, soundly beaten and on the run, even honor a white flag at this stage of the game? He had personally witnessed Germans firing on other Americans in similar situations. The Germans were fifty yards away now. Captain Brown asked, "What do we do, sir?"

The colonel replied, "Pray, Captain. Pray like you've never prayed before."

The Americans watched the approaching enemy who would at any moment begin firing into the grass and weeds in search of the prey they knew were hiding somewhere along that ditch.

Captain Brown made the Sign of the Cross and began to whisper, "Hail Mary, full of grace . . ." The others began making their peace with their God in their own way. The situation appeared hopeless. At any moment they were all going to die.

Young Johnathan Howard, a twenty-year-old soldier from Omaha, Nebraska, gasped and pointed to a spot in the road between them and the oncoming Germans. Everyone looked up to see a small white cloud that had suddenly appeared, hovering a few feet above the ground in the center of the road. The cloud remained motionless for a few seconds, then began to fade. As it did, the dust in the road started to twirl in a circular motion. The cloud was suddenly gone, replaced now by a rising whirlwind that had erupted in the very center of the road and effectively screened Fry and his men from the advancing Germans.

Fry and the others were momentarily mesmerized by the sight. The whirlwind stretched the width of the road and rose in a vertical column to a height of over fifty feet and remained stationary in that very spot, blocking them from the view of the Germans, who were now cursing and shouting excitedly.

"There's our smokescreen, boys," shouted Fry, "and it's God-sent. Get those jeeps turned around."

The road was narrow, so turning the jeeps around took time. Each had to be backed up twice before the turn could be accomplished. All that time, the whirlwind remained in exactly the same spot, concealing the Americans' activity.

With everyone aboard, the drivers went full throttle and the jeeps raced for friendly territory. As they went around a bend, Colonel Fry looked back over his shoulder and saw the whirlwind column still in place. Later, asking about his experience, a group of fellow officers wanted to know to what he attributed this strange occurrence. Was it chance? Luck? Or simply a freak of nature?

He quickly answered, "Gentlemen, Mr. Webster's fine dictionary defines a whirlwind as a current of air whirling violently in a spiral form and having a forward motion.

"There was not a breath of air moving in the valley that day, and the whirlwind we observed never moved one foot to the left or right, nor did it move forward or backward. I will only say that we all asked for divine intervention in a very bad situation and that plea was answered."

One of the officers asked, "Corporal Howard believes that the small cloud that you saw before the whirlwind was actually an angel. Do you believe that?"

"I will not question that, sir. Clearly, there was someone with us that day that no one saw."

Colonel James Fry went on to serve his country with the utmost honor, retiring as a major general from the United States army.

Corporal Johnathan Howard left the army after the war and had been so moved by the experience of that day that he joined the ministry. He has spent the last forty-five years preaching the word of God and the wonderful work of His angels.

## 17

# And the Bible Told Him So

WITH THE BOMBING OF PEARL HARBOR, AMERICA WAS launched full-force into a world war. Although the American Navy was seriously crippled by the Japanese attack at Hawaii, American determination and industrial mobilization quickly set into motion a giant war machine geared to turn the tide on the attackers.

Plenty of battles were fought against the Japanese in the Pacific, however, historians agree that none had a more decisive effect in that area than the battle for Guadalcanal.

This bloody campaign was fought on and around an island few Americans had ever heard of—an island ninety miles long and twenty-five miles wide, yet twenty-six thousand men would fall on this small piece of real estate that would become known as a pestilential hell on earth.

Going into this meat-grinder battle, the U.S. Marines would receive an early lesson in the fanatical methods of bravery and tenacity of which the Japanese soldier was capable when trapped and left with no recourse but to surrender or die.

Among the young men who would soon test those imperial Japanese troops was Corporal William Devers, First Battalion, Fifth Marines. A twenty-one-year-old from Tulsa, Oklahoma, who listed his religion as "none," Corporal Devers was an agnostic.

Now an agnostic is not to be confused with an atheist. An atheist flatly denies the very existence of God or any other divine being, whereas an agnostic believes it is impossible to know anything about God or the creation of the universe and refrains from committing himself to any religious order or belief. Agnosticism is not a flat denial of God.

Knowing of Devers's belief, a number of his fellow Marines set about to change the corporal's mind about God. But no amount of arguing, Bible quoting, or coercion could sway the young Marine. A few members of the unit began to warn others to distance themselves from the nonbeliever when they hit the beaches, for he was sure to be one of the first to die.

This kind of talk did not seem to bother the corporal, but one person was concerned: Captain Francis E. Hand, the First Battalion chaplain. He had observed the efforts of the other Marines to convert the young agnostic and had elected not to interfere, hoping instead that Devers would come to him to discuss the matter. However, as time went on, the corporal showed no such interest.

On the night before they were to depart New Zealand for some still-unknown island, the chaplain asked Corporal Devers to join him for a walk on the deck of their troopship. It was an invitation that the corporal had been expecting for some time.

The two men talked about home, family, and

friends for a while before the chaplain went straight
to the matter of God. Devers, respectful of the man's
rank rather than his profession, explained his reasons
for his belief, citing a number of supernatural happenings in the Bible as reason enough to question
the book's validity.

Surprised, Hand asked, "Oh, then you have read
the Bible?"

"Yes," answered Devers. "Enough of it to know
that it asks you to believe a lot of things that can't
be logically explained."

"Then you don't believe the Bible to be a true
story?"

"No, sir, I'm sorry. I just don't buy it."

The chaplain stood silent for a moment, then
asked, "Do you still have a Bible, Corporal
Devers?"

"No, sir," replied the boy, explaining that he had
lost the one he had been given at the reception station
a long time ago, but that it didn't matter because he
didn't need one anyway.

The chaplain withdrew a small Bible from his shirt
pocket and offered it to Devers. "Here, take this one,
son. I have more than enough of them—even for the
nonbelievers."

Devers refused, again stating that he had no need
for a Bible. Saluting, he politely excused himself and
returned below deck, leaving the chaplain standing
alone at the ship's railing to ponder their discussion.

At 0900 hours, July 22, 1942, the Marines departed New Zealand and began the journey that
would take them to the shores of a small island
called Guadalcanal.

At 0613 on the morning of August 7, the first
salvos of naval gunfire arched into the beaches of

that deadly island and America began its march to repel the Japanese and drive them back to Japan. As the chaplain watched elements of the Second Marines go over the side to launch the initial attack against the smaller island of Tulagi, he noticed Corporal Devers standing one deck below, also watching the activity. Catching the young man's eye, Chaplain Hand raised a small Bible in the air and nodded toward the boy. Devers smiled kindly, but again refused the chaplain's offer.

By 0930 it was the First Battalion's turn to go over the side and into the LCPs that would take them to the beaches of Guadalcanal. Surprisingly, reports of enemy resistance were almost nonexistent. This made more than a few members of the high command nervous. Where were the Japanese?

Moving ashore without a shot being fired, Devers grinned at the chaplain as he came by and remarked, "You see, Chaplain, it all worked out okay without me carrying a Bible."

Before Hand could reply, Devers waved good-bye and took off to join his squad, which was moving into the jungle. Tapping the small Bible in his shirt pocket, Chaplain Hand made a silent vow to himself that before they left this island he would convince Corporal Devers that the Bible was more than just a well-written book of fairy tales that the boy perceived it to be.

The chaplain did not encounter Devers again until the morning of the nineteenth. A large Japanese force had been sighted near a village. Two companies of the Fifth were to attack the enemy and secure prisoners for interrogation. This would be the unit's first all-out encounter with a sizable Japanese force, and many of the men were relieved to see that Chaplain

Hand had volunteered to go along with them on the operation. Seeing Devers near the point element, the chaplain made his way to him and was about to relate a dream he had had the previous night, but before he could do so, the platoon leader gave the order to move out for the objective.

Making their way through the jungle for over a mile, the unit turned east for another seven hundred yards and found the village. Moving quietly into position, they caught the Japanese totally by surprise. In a bitterly contested battle, the Marines overpowered the enemy force, killing all but ten, while sustaining losses of four killed and eleven wounded.

Escorting one of the prisoners to a containment area, Devers saw the chaplain kneeling over a seriously wounded Marine. A shot suddenly rang out and Chaplain Hand was knocked backward into the dirt, a red stain spreading rapidly over the right side of his utility jacket.

"Sniper!" yelled someone.

Pushing the POW to the ground, Devers rushed to the chaplain's side. Although clearly in great pain, Chaplain Hand managed to say, "My . . . left pocket . . . Take it . . . please."

Devers reached into the wounded man's shirt pocket and removed the small Bible. Looking at it for a moment, he commented, "I'm not so sure, Chaplain. No disrespect, but it don't seem to have done you much good."

Struggling to hold back his pain, Hand replied, "Last night, I had a dream. In the dream . . . an angel appeared and told me that I had to make you take that Bible. Take it, son . . . please."

Devers hesitated for a moment, then shoved the Bible into his shirt pocket to satisfy the wounded man. Within minutes, the sniper had been dispatched by a rifle squad, and the corpsmen were at the chaplain's side administering morphine. The bullet had broken the chaplain's right collarbone—painful, but he would live.

As the morphine injection began to take hold, the chaplain squeezed Corporal Devers's hand. "Angels are not to be taken lightly, my boy. They are God's messengers. They rejoice when a nonbeliever is converted to His word. Remember that."

Devers nodded and walked away, convinced that the remarks were merely the words of a wounded man under the influence of morphine. Angels and dreams, thought the young marine. More fairy-tale stuff, but Chaplain Hand was a good man, and if taking the Bible would somehow comfort him, then so be it.

The village and the prisoners secured, the Marines began their trip back to their main base. Corporal Devers's squad was on the point. They had been traveling for about twenty minutes when they rounded a bend in the trail and stumbled right into a Japanese patrol. A sudden, violent firefight erupted at very close range. Two Marines on Devers's right went down. Another on his left was killed instantly. Devers, his heart pounding, fired into the Japanese until his rifle was empty.

Desperately, he tried to reload the weapon. A sudden impact knocked him off his feet. His chest felt as if a tree had fallen on him and his mind began to fade into darkness. William Devers was certain he was dying.

What seemed to the young Marine to be a lifetime was, in fact, only a matter of a few minutes. When he opened his eyes he found the five remaining members of his squad kneeling around him.

"What happened?" he asked.

One of the Marines who had tried his hand at converting the agnostic in New Zealand smiled and held up the small Bible that the chaplain had urged him to take. There was an ugly-looking hole in the cover. "I didn't realize agnostics had the privilege of having guardian angels," said the Marine holding the Bible.

Sitting up, Devers felt a ripple of pain shoot through the right side of his chest, but there was no blood. "What are you talking about?" asked a confused Devers.

Passing the Bible to the young agnostic, the Marine replied, "I think someone you're not sure exists is trying to tell you something, Billy boy."

William Devers stared at the hole in the book for a moment, then opened it. A bullet from a Japanese officer's pistol had torn through the Bible, ending its journey at the book of Psalms, 91:7, which read, "A thousand shall fall at thy side, and ten thousand at thy right hand; but it shall not come nigh thee."

Captain Francis E. Hand recovered from his wound and joined to another Marine unit in the Pacific. Six months after his return, he was administering the last rites to a wounded Marine inside a makeshift tent hospital on another island when an enemy plane strafed the facility. Chaplain Hand was among those killed. He had died doing what he loved best, providing God's words of comfort to those in need.

Corporal William Devers survived the war and returned to Tulsa, Oklahoma, where he married and began a prosperous construction business. When he died in the summer of 1989, he was best remembered by friends and neighbors for his unselfish devotion of time and service to his church, in particular, the time he spent talking with young people who had doubts about the stories in the Bible.

His daughter, Frances, still has the small Bible that saved her father's life that day. It is encased in glass and stands opened to the book of Psalms. The left side clearly shows the bullet hole, and on the right side there is a small indentation where the bullet stopped at the beginning of Psalms 91:7.

Did an angel's appearance in Chaplain Hand's dream save the life of William Devers?

## 18

# The Midway Miracle

IN THE PREDAWN DARKNESS OF JUNE 4, 1942, LIEUTENant Commander Jason W. Phillips, a navy pilot aboard the aircraft carrier U.S.S. *Enterprise,* strolled the deck of the massive carrier and stared out at the first gray lines of morning that seemed to be rising from the very depths of the Pacific Ocean.

Somewhere out there in the vastness of that ocean was a Japanese naval force three times larger than the one that had attacked Pearl Harbor on December 7, 1941. They were commanded by Admiral Isoroku Yamamoto, the architect of the December 7 attack that had all but devastated America's naval power.

Yamamoto hoped that by seizing Midway Island, he could draw what remained of the American Pacific fleet away from Hawaii and into a decisive sea battle where his superior strength in numbers could destroy the remnants of the American navy, thereby giving Japan total control of the Pacific and opening the way for a full-scale invasion of the Hawaiian Islands.

What Admiral Yamamoto did not know was that American intelligence had broken the Japanese codes since the attack on Pearl Harbor. This stroke of genius, or luck, whichever you prefer, proved invaluable to the Americans. Immediately, America's meager but determined armada of three aircraft carriers set a course to intercept the Japanese fleet, knowing full well that their only chance of winning the battle depended on total surprise. They would have to locate the enemy and strike a critical first blow against the Japanese before they could retaliate.

Two men who would play principal parts in the coming battle were Lieutenant Commander Phillips, a bomber pilot, and his navigator/radioman, Ensign T. J. Powell. Both men had met at flight school and had managed to stay together since graduating. They made a perfect team when flying their Devastator bomber.

On the morning of June 3, the aircraft carrier *Yorktown* had launched its search planes, hoping to find the exact location of the Japanese fleet and radio the information back to the American command. But as daylight began to fade, Yamamoto's force had not been located and the search planes returned to the *Yorktown*.

Just before dawn on the fourth, the *Yorktown* launched ten planes, again to search out the enemy. Twice the pilot crews of the carrier *Enterprise* manned their planes on false alarms, and both times they were recalled to the ready room to wait for the launch order.

Tension was running high among the pilots, as well as every member of the American task force. After the second recall, Lieutenant Commander Phillips requested that he be allowed to remain above deck for a while. He had begun to feel as if the cramped quarters of the ready room were closing in around him. The flight commander granted his request.

Around 0530 hours, Ensign Powell joined his friend and pilot on the flight line. The two talked quietly about home and their folks, friends, and girlfriends. Eventually, the discussion came around to God and the chance that this could be the last sunrise either of them might ever see.

Ensign Thomas Johnathan Powell was twenty-one years old and a native of Bristol, Tennessee. His mother had raised seven children by herself. Although they had been poor and lacked a lot of material things, their mother had been a solid Christian woman who taught her children the power of the Bible and the word of God.

Lieutenant Commander Phillips, on the other hand, was twenty-five years old, engaged to be married, and somewhat reluctant to discuss religious matters. Not because he didn't believe, but mainly because religion was just something from which he had gradually drifted away over the years. Would the Lord hold that against him? he asked his friend.

Powell laughed and assured him that as long as he believed in his heart, he would have the protection of the angels.

Phillips wanted to pursue that theory, but before he had the chance, another alarm sounded and the two scrambled down to the ready room, where intelligence officers quickly gave them a final briefing. After a short verse from the chaplain, the crews rushed out of the ready room and headed for the flight deck.

Their faces were boyish in the growing morning

light and each showed a fringe of peach fuzz; it was their ritual not to shave until a battle was ended. The flight crews' close buddies, the ground crews, had finished checking, arming, fueling, and servicing the planes.

The young pilots climbed into their weapons of war casually. Nonchalance was the order of the day; no good for a man to betray nervousness or tension, that was considered very bad form. They warmed their engines while planes that had already launched circled in the sky above the *Enterprise*.

There was hand signaling to the deck directors, a casual wave to a wing man whom they might never see again. The launch director raised his arms. The pilots revved their engines to maximum, then one by one throttled forward and streaked off the steel island for the sky above to join the formation overhead— and soon, perhaps, the heavenly feathered choir.

While Lieutenant Commander Phillips and his flight were making their way toward the Japanese task force, fifteen torpedo bombers from the aircraft carrier *Hornet,* mistakenly believing they had carrier fighter support flying high above them, went in for the attack. Flying through swarms of Japanese fighters that seem to come from everywhere at once, the *Hornet* bombers continued to lumber their slow-moving planes straight at one of the lead enemy carriers. Antiaircraft fire was so intense that it seared faces and tore huge chunks out of the planes. One by one the brave crews were torn apart. Ironically, those few who made it close enough to release their torpedoes before they were blown apart were spared the sight of their bombs striking the target, then sinking harmlessly into the sea—the detonators on their torpedoes were faulty. In less than ten minutes, all fifteen planes were shot down. Of the thirty men from the *Hornet* flight, only one survived.

At 0950, Lieutenant Commander Phillips's flight had been joined by a flight from the *Yorktown*. The two squadrons banked over and came screaming downward at a seventy-degree angle, with speeds rising to 335 miles per hour. The Japanese were taken completely by surprise. They were still trying to straighten their course after the attack of the *Hornet* squadron, and their fighter planes were just then beginning to climb toward combat altitude when the bombs struck the Japanese carriers like a sledgehammer.

Coming in low, Phillips released his bombs right over the flight deck of the lead Japanese carrier. Ensign Powell watched it penetrate the first deck before it exploded in the lower hangar area. Letting out a yell, he screamed into his radio, "We got a hit! We got a direct hit, skipper!"

Phillips was overjoyed at the news. Pulling up and going for altitude, he suddenly found himself face to face with an oncoming Japanese fighter. The Japanese Zero's guns were flashing as a hail of bullets tore through the windshield of the Devastator. Screaming pain gripped Phillips as slivers of glass penetrated both of his eyes and everything went black. Lieutenant Commander Phillips was blind.

In panic, Phillips called to his radioman. "T.J.— T.J.! Are you all right? Answer me, T.J.! My God— I'm blind! I can't see!"

The wounded pilot called back to his friend and navigator once more, but there was no reply. A long moment passed, then a voice came over the radio. It wasn't the voice of Ensign Powell. It sounded more like that of Lieutenant Commander Neal McCormick, another pilot in the flight. He was screaming for Phillips to pull up.

Phillips, in agonizing pain, pulled back on the stick and felt the nose of the aircraft lift skyward. He tried to wipe at the blood coming from his eyes, but the pain was too intense.

McCormick was on the radio again telling Phillips to bring the stick forward. He would tell him when he was leveled off. Phillips did as instructed, easing the stick forward until McCormick told him to stop. "Can you talk to your navigator?" asked McCormick. "Negative," came the reply.

McCormick's voice came over Phillips's headsets in a calm and comforting manner. "Don't worry, Jason. I'll get you home. Just do as I say, when I say, and you'll make it fine, okay? Now start turning to the right until I tell you to stop."

Phillips did as instructed. The next order was to climb for altitude. Again Phillips complied. For the next forty-five minutes, Phillips flew his crippled aircraft, going only on the voice commands of McCormick.

In the silent periods between commands, Phillips quietly muttered the only prayer that he knew. The Twenty-third Psalm: " 'The Lord is my shepherd; I shall not want. He maketh me to lie down in green pastures; he leadeth me beside the still waters. He restoreth my soul; he leadeth me in the paths of righteousness for his name's sake.' " At that point Phillips stopped. It had been so long since he had prayed, he had forgotten the rest of the words.

McCormick's voice came softly through the headset, " 'Yea, though I walk through the valley of the shadow of death, I will fear no evil: for thou art with me; thy rod and thy staff they comfort me. . . .' "

Lieutenant Commander Jason Phillips felt a sudden peace come over him as he completed the rest of the verse by himself. Five minutes later, McCormick was on the radio again. Their aircraft carrier was in sight. Now came the hard part: landing on the deck of a steel-plated, bobbing island in the middle of the ocean. The peace Phillips had known only minutes ago began to give way to fear and apprehension. He wasn't going to make it. Landing on a carrier was hard enough for a man with two good eyes. For a blind man, it was impossible. His voice trembling, he relayed these fears to McCormick.

The reply was totally unexpected. " 'For he shall give his angels charge over thee, to keep thee in all thy ways.' "

Lieutenant Commander Phillips again felt the calm come over him as he repeated the words to himself and listened to McCormick's commands. "Ease to the left . . . that's it. A little more. Okay. Now start your descent . . . easy . . . easy . . . easy . . . okay. A little more right . . . that's it. Now start easing the stick down. That's good."

Calmly the voice lined up the crippled aircraft on the one and only approach the wounded pilot would get.

"Okay, you're on line," said the voice. "When I tell you to drop it, you push the stick all the way forward and cut the engine."

Phillips tried to answer but his mouth had gone to cotton. He listened intently for the command. When it came, he shoved the stick forward, cutting the engine at the same instant. The plane dropped like a rock, bounced once, twice, then the tailhook caught the cable. The sudden jerking motion threw the pilot forward into the instrument panel, knocking him unconscious. Lieutenant Commander Phillips was home.

The carrier crewmen swarmed over the bullet-riddled aircraft, carefully removed the two occupants, and rushed them below to the medical room and a team of waiting doctors.

It was three days before Phillips woke from his ordeal. His eyes were heavily bandaged and his entire body ached, but he was alive. His first question to his doctor was about the condition of his friend Ensign Powell. The doctor informed him that his navigator had died instantly from two bullet wounds to the head, inflicted by the same plane that had blinded Phillips.

Now the doctor had a question. How had Phillips managed to fly a plane that had been shot to pieces, and then land that same plane on a carrier while blind?

Phillips related the details of his ordeal to the doctor, who sat spellbound by the story. When he had finished, Phillips requested that the doctor please let Lieutenant Commander McCormick know that he would like to see him to personally thank him for saving his life.

Still stunned by the story, the doctor finally managed to speak. "Lieutenant Commander Phillips, I am afraid that will not be possible. Lieutenant Commander McCormick's plane was one of the first ones in your flight to go down in the attack on the Japanese carrier. Both he and his navigator were killed."

"That's not possible," said a shaken Phillips. "He was talking to me on the radio just before I landed. The radio room ... the bridge, they had to hear the radio traffic. Didn't they hear us talking?"

The doctor placed his hand on Phillips's shoulder

"Now, relax, Commander. We did hear you on the radio. That's how we knew you were in trouble. We heard you praying just before you landed. But there was only one voice, son. We didn't hear anyone else."

Giving Phillips a sedative to relax him, the doctor told him to rest. He would have to give a full report when he felt better. Phillips didn't answer. He was still in shock at the news about McCormick. Leaving the room, the doctor said, "I don't know how, or who, guided you home, son. But what you did was a true miracle."

Was this a true miracle? If you're not sure, close your eyes and try to walk across a room, then think of trying to land a crippled plane on a strip of steel in the middle of an ocean with your eyes closed.

If Ensign Powell was killed instantly, and Lieutenant Commander McCormick went down at the battle site, who spoke to Lieutenant Commander Phillips? Who gave him directions and instructions? Who comforted him in his time of fear?

For those who believe, the answer is an easy one. For those who do not, how can they answer these questions?

Lieutenant Commander Jason Phillips regained partial sight a few years later, but was deemed legally blind. He returned home to a hero's welcome and was an early pioneer in lobbying for the handicapped. Upon his death in 1982, his church purchased a polished marble headstone adorned with an angel. Etched below his name are the words, "For he shall give his angels charge over thee . . ."

# 19

# *The Miracle of the Rain*

THE FOLLOWING IS A STORY THAT BEGAN ON OCTOBER 21, 1942. The participants were members of the United States Army Air Corps, Transport Command, and one famous American civilian.

The Transport Command had the duty of flying newly constructed aircraft to forward operations areas in the Pacific and returning to the States with the older aircraft that had been replaced. On this particular flight, the pilot was Captain William T. Cherry. His co-pilot was Lieutenant James C. Whittaker; Second Lieutenant John J. DeAngelis was the navigator; Staff Sergeant James W. Reynolds was the radio operator; and Corporal Johnny Bartek was the flight engineer.

Bill Cherry's crew was returning from a forward base where they had delivered a new B-17 bomber. They were now on the return trip, and after a stopover at Hickam Field in Hawaii, they would be headed home to the States.

On the morning of the nineteenth, they arrived at the field to find that their orders had been changed. They and their Flying Fortress had been reassigned to carry the famous Captain Eddie Rickenbacker and an aide on a secret mission for the War Department. The crew was disappointed, of course. They had hoped to be home in a few hours, but orders were orders. Besides, they all wanted to meet the World War I ace who had knocked down twenty-six German planes and had become a hero in that war.

The famous visitor arrived at the runway at ten-thirty the following day. Rickenbacker was now a civilian, and Washington had insisted that he have a military aide with him. The man he had chosen was Colonel Hans Adamson, a friend from his World War I days. Accompanying them was Sergeant Alex Kaczmarczyk, another flight engineer, who had been released from the base hospital and was returning to his unit.

Things immediately began to go wrong. As Captain Cherry headed the huge Fortress down the runway to takeoff, a cable in the brake assembly broke, sending the plane into a sideways skid. Cherry groundlooped the plane a few times before bringing it safely to a stop. Rickenbacker complimented him on his excellent reaction and left the plane with his aide. Cherry went about checking on his crew. Everyone was all right, but he noticed Lieutenant DeAngelis checking his octant, which had flown across his plotting board and hit the side of the aircraft. (An octant is an optical instrument similar to a sextant. It is employed in navigation to measure angles and distances and ascertain latitudes and longitudes.)

"Equipment all right?" asked Cherry.

"As far as I can tell," replied DeAngelis.

An inspection of the damaged aircraft determined that repairs were out of the question. They would have to take another plane. It was well after midnight by the time all equipment and personnel gear had been switched over to the new aircraft. They departed Hickam Field at one twenty-nine A.M., October 21.

For the first few hours everything seemed to be all right, but soon DeAngelis came up to the cockpit with a worried look on his face. They had passed their ETA (estimated time of arrival) and there was no island in sight. The octant had given them a false reading. By the time they realized the malfunction, they were down to four hours of fuel. In Captain Cherry's words, "We were totally lost."

Whittaker and Cherry agreed that they would have to fly a box pattern—in other words, make a turn, fly one hour, then make another turn for another hour, then turn again, and so forth until they completed a box pattern. By doing this they hoped by chance to spot the island—or any island, for that matter.

In the meantime, Rickenbacker organized the crew and the equipment that would be needed should they have to ditch. By the time they had made the last turn, it became apparent that there were no islands in their area and they were going to have to crash-land in the sea.

A talented pilot, Captain Cherry brought the giant Fortress in at just the right level and pancaked it across the waves with minimum damage. Immediately three life rafts were inflated and the crew abandoned ship. All told, there were eight men in the three rafts. However, the plane had begun to fill with water so fast that the person designated to recover the food and water had forgotten those two precious items in his rush to exit the sinking aircraft. The only food they had when the plane went beneath the waves were four oranges found bobbing in the water.

Staff Sergeant Reynolds had sent out SOS signals over his radio until the very last minute. As the sun set on their first night, the survivors were not overly concerned. They were certain the signal had been heard and that once they were discovered to be over-due at the island, an immediate search would begin. Cherry busied himself taking inventory of what they had saved. There were two air pumps for the rafts, two knives, three Very pistols with eighteen flares (half of which turned out to be duds), two .45-caliber pistols, oars, some fish hooks, and some line.

The second day passed and there were no signs of search aircraft. Still they were not overly worried. There was a war going on, after all, and a rescue would take considerable organizing.

By the third day, the men began to realize the hardships facing them. From about eleven in the morning until four in the afternoon, the sun bore down on them as if they were ants on a huge griddle, cooking them unmerciful. That night, the waves rose to heights of ten to twelve feet, tossing them about and covering them with spray and mist that became unbelievably cold during the early morning hours. Each man was soon hoping for the heat of the sun.

By the fourth day food was becoming a major concern. The small pieces of orange that were passed out each day did little to sustain them. It was after-noon when Staff Sergeant Reynolds remembered the fish hooks and line. Captain Cherry used an orange peel for bait, but after a few hours realized that fish were not attracted to the peeling.

On the fifth day Cherry made another attempt with the peeling and again found it useless. The discussion suddenly went to more formidable bait. When Cherry asked aloud if fingernail parings would work, Johnny Bartek replied, "Naw, the only thing we've got for bait is our hides."

Everyone went quiet. This presented a startling possibility.

"What part would you use?" asked Whittaker.

"The earlobe," said Bartek. "You don't need it and you wouldn't miss it."

"How about the ball of the little finger?" said Whittaker. "A small slice wouldn't cause much pain and there would be little chance of infection."

"I think a piece of toe would do," said Reynolds. "That way no one would ever know you'd been disfigured."

As terrible as this conversation may sound, the reader must remember that these men were growing weaker with each passing hour. They would have to have food soon if they were to stand any chance of survival. However, the part of the anatomy that they would have selected will never be known. For a few moments after the others asked Captain Rickenbacker's opinion, a startling event occurred.

Just before, the air above them had been void of anything but the burning sun. Now there was a loud flapping of wings. Totally without warning and seemingly coming from nowhere, a sea swallow landed on Eddie Rickenbacker's head. A bird about half the size of a seagull, the sea swallow sat precariously on Rickenbacker's head and stared at each man with understandable curiosity.

Slowly, Rickenbacker moved his hand up to his chin, then along his eyebrow. No one in the boat breathed. In one quick motion, Rickenbacker snatched the bird from his head. Holding it firmly, he began to tear it apart and divide it among the starving men.

Where had this bird come from? Whittaker himself estimated that the box pattern they had flown revealed that there were no land masses within a 165-square-mile radius of where their plane went down. Yet this small bird appeared from nowhere to provide the desperate men with a small amount of food, but more importantly, with the bait they needed for their hooks.

Within minutes of eating the sea swallow, they caught two fair-sized fish. As the fish were being prepared for distribution, young Johnny Bartek unzipped his small New Testament and gave a silent prayer of thanks.

Whittaker noticed this and commented, ''Do you think that had anything to do with the bird, Bartek?''

The airman nodded and replied, ''The Lord's angels can appear in many shapes and forms, Lieutenant Whittaker.''

The lieutenant started to criticize the statement, but let it go for the time being.

By the sixth day, water was becoming a critical need. That afternoon, Bartek removed his small Bible and asked if the others would mind pulling the three rafts, which were attached by a line, together so that they could hold a prayer meeting.

Lieutenant Whittaker commented in his book, *We Thought We Heard the Angels Sing,* that he had been exposed to religion and Bible teachings at an early age, but had long ago lost any interest in such things. When Bartek began reciting the Lord's Prayer, Whittaker could only remember a word here and there.

He never seriously thought that the open-air revival meeting was going to do much good. But they were in trouble, there was no denying that, so what harm could it do?

Colonel Adamson, Rickenbacker's aide, volunteered to read at this first meeting. Thumbing through the small Bible, the colonel found the Scripture he was searching for. It was Matthew 6:31–34. In a reverent tone that seemed natural to the man, he began to read aloud.

" 'Therefore take no thought, saying, What shall we eat? or, What shall we drink? or, Wherewithal shall we be clothed? (For after all these things do the Gentiles seek:) for your heavenly Father knoweth that you have need of all these things. But seek ye first the kingdom of God, and his righteousness; and all these things shall be added unto you. Take therefore no thought for the morrow: for the morrow shall take thought for the things of itself. Sufficient unto the day is the evil thereof.' "

When he had finished, Whittaker was surprised to find himself rather impressed and said so aloud, adding that the evil had certainly been sufficient unto the last few days.

The colonel quickly explained that these verses did not mean tomorrow literally, that perhaps they meant soon.

Whittaker thought of the words all through the cold, wet, dreary night that followed, finally dismissing them with the decision that he would "believe" when he saw the food and water. Whittaker would not have to wait long. He would receive a sample of startling proof the following night.

The sweltering sun beat down on the group as they drifted into their seventh day on the sea. The last orange was carefully divided and its minimal liquid was gone in seconds, leaving Whittaker even thirstier than before. His hopes stirred the previous night had now vanished in the face of hard reality.

By the time the evening prayer session began, Whittaker's cynicism had reached epic proportions. As Colonel Adamson began to read, Whittaker thought to himself how ridiculous it appeared for men as practical and as hardboiled as these to expect a mumbling voice bobbing about in the middle of an ocean to summon help for them.

When the colonel had finished, Captain Cherry repeated the passage from Matthew about the food and water on the morrow.

"Yeah, always tomorrow," thought Whittaker bitterly.

Captain Cherry then began his own version of a prayer, referring to God as the Old Master. He spoke simply and directly.

"Old Master, we know this isn't a guarantee we'll eat in the morning, but we're in an awful fix, as you know. We sure are counting on a little something by day after tomorrow, at least. Please see what you can do for us, Old Master."

Finishing his prayer, Cherry fired off a flare just as they had done each evening, in the hope that someone would see it. This time the flare's charge was faulty and the fireball rose only fifty feet or so into the air, then fell back among the rafts. It hissed and zigzagged in the water like a small red snake, giving off a brilliant red light, illuminating the sea for a hundred yards. In the glow the men could see a school of fish attracted by the light. They were being pursued by a number of barracuda.

Two large fish, fleeing one of the razor-mouthed

predators, suddenly broke the surface of the water and dived straight into one of the rafts. The men only had seconds to grab them before the flare faded and darkness closed in around them. Once again, food had been provided.

By the eighth day, water became more important than food. On this afternoon, Captain Cherry again called on the Old Master.

"Old Master, we called upon you for food and you delivered. We ask you now for water. We've done the best we could. If you don't make up your mind to help us pretty soon, I guess that's all there'll be to it. It looks like the next move's up to you, Old Master."

It was a prayer that had everything a prayer should have: a petition to God, an expressed resignation to God's will, and the belief—the faith—that the petition would be answered.

As the rafts drifted apart, Whittaker thought to himself that if God ever wanted to make a believer out of Lieutenant James C. Whittaker, this was the time for it.

His thoughts continued along that line for a while. It wasn't until he looked off to his left that he saw what had earlier been a bank of fleecy white clouds. They were darkening by the second.

He shouted, drawing the attention of the others to the beautiful sight. They all watched in silence as a bluish curtain unrolled slowly from the cloud to the sea. It was rain—and it was carrying straight for the rafts. Prayers rose from the excited group. It was less than a quarter mile away when a perverse wind suddenly rose and began pushing the curtain away from them.

For the first time, Lieutenant Whittaker found himself leading the group in prayer. Not sure what to say, he simply began, "God, you know what that water means to us. The wind has blown it away. It is in your power, God, to send back that rain. It's nothing to you, but it means life to us."

Some of the others had already given up, saying that the wind would blow in that direction for the next forty years. But Whittaker wasn't about to give up. He had already seen things happen that had renewed a long-lost faith within him. Now, shouting with all the strength he could force from his lungs, the lieutenant screamed, "God, the wind is yours. You own it. It is in your power to have your angels bring that rain back to us, your children, who shall surely die without it."

Now, there are some things in this modern world that defy all the rules of logic or nature. What occurred that day in the middle of the Pacific Ocean was witnessed by every man present, including the highly respected Captain Eddie Rickenbacker, a man whose character was without reproach.

No sooner had Lieutenant Whittaker finished his heartfelt appeal than the curtain of rain stopped exactly where it was. However, the wind did not change direction, nor did it decrease in velocity. Nonetheless, the curtain of life-giving rain, ever so slowly, began to move back toward the rafts—against the wind.

In all, the men survived twenty-one days of their torturous ordeal before being rescued. One of their number, Sergeant Kaczmarczyk, who had been released from the hospital the day before the flight had departed and who had not been in top physical condition, lost his battle with the harsh elements during the rigorous ordeal.

In the end, one cannot help wondering about the

mystery of the events that these brave men experienced. The sudden appearance of a sea swallow? Fish jumping into a raft? A curtain of rain defying nature itself and moving against the wind?

If you were to ask Lieutenant James C. Whittaker to explain these happenings to you, his answer would be the same one that he gave thousands of others as he traveled the country raising money for the war by promoting war bonds.

"God and his corps of angels reminded us that they are always with us. We have only to ask for their help."

# THE
# KOREAN WAR

JUNE 25, 1950, WAS A NORMAL SATURDAY IN AMERICA. Kids rode their bikes while Dad washed the car and Mom worked on her flower beds. It had been five years since the end of the "big war"—World War II. Thoughts of another war were the farthest thing from any American's mind that warm Saturday afternoon. President Harry S Truman had even left the White House to spend a little vacation time at his home in Independence, Missouri.

In Tokyo, Douglas MacArthur, an American hero and one of the president's top generals, was sound asleep. North Korea's military leaders were also sleeping, confident that they had done all that could be done to make the proper reply to the United Nations' latest peace proposal.

Along the 38th Parallel, the two-hundred-mile armed border that separated North and South Korea, it was raining. The summer monsoons had begun, making it a miserable night for the South Korean soldiers on guard duty along the border.

In the distance, they thought they heard the murmur of thunder in the mountains to the north. It wasn't the sound of thunder, but the rumble of artillery. At exactly four o'clock in the morning the first shells of the Democratic People's Republic of Korea struck their brothers in the South. The conflict in Korea had began.

The Korean war is the stepchild of America's wars. It is not as famous as the Civil War, or the war to end all wars. And it is nowhere near the greatness of the "big one"—World War II. No, the Korean war is none of these things. To Americans it was just some little Asian country fighting with its neighbor over villages, towns, and cities with names no one could pronounce. It went on practically unnoticed by anyone except those who had to fight it and the families who were to grieve because they did.

These are but a few of the stories of that little-known war and of a few men who found themselves on those wind-swept ridges, feeling totally alone . . . or so they believed . . .

## 20

# The Angel and Mr. Smith

Writ in the climate of heaven,
in the language spoken by angels.

—HENRY WADSWORTH LONGFELLOW

BAKER COMPANY, THIRD PLATOON COMMANDED BY Second Lieutenant Ryan Bressler, with forty-two men, manned Outpost Dale. It was a small hill at the terminus of a larger ridge's farthest extended finger. The larger ridge lying six hundred yards behind Dale was the company command post under the command of First Lieutenant Jack Patterson and the remaining 144 men of Baker Company, forty of whom were newly arrived South Korean replacements.

Approximately four hundred yards straight across from Baker Company was a massive hill designated Hill 222. It was garrisoned by a Chinese company of hard-core Communist troops. Between these two enemies ran a narrow valley pockmarked with craters and studded with blasted and twisted tree stumps. Under the full moon these trees shone like silver sentinels to the men in the forward position of Outpost Dale.

For the men of the Third Platoon it was watch night. Military intelligence had reported a flurry of activity during the day coming from Hill 222. It was highly possible that Baker Company could expect a visit from their neighbors across the way before the night was over.

It was 2300 hours (eleven P.M. civilian time), and so far the night had been uneventful. Anxiety kept the newly arrived replacements wide awake, their eyes searching every shadow and their ears picking up the slightest sound, real or imagined. The seasoned veterans, made skeptical by frequent experiences with false alarms, were more relaxed, many taking advantage of the stillness to catch a few minutes of sleep here and there. They had already learned the hard way: You sleep whenever or wherever you can. It may be a long time before you get another chance.

Positioned forward of and below the ridge of Outpost Dale, twelve men of Baker Company were paired in six foxhole listening posts that formed a rough crescent around the lower slopes.

Twenty-year-old Private First Class Joseph Smith from Claxton, Georgia, had been with the company only five days. He had been paired with another new arrival, nineteen-year-old Lee Chang Woo, a South Korean private who had been in the army less than thirty days. Mere chance and the luck of the draw had placed these two men in position at Listening Post 21 that night.

Private Smith was grateful that Private Woo spoke

English, having been taught by missionaries at an orphanage in Seoul that had been Woo's home since the age of six. Early on in their watch the two young men scanned the terrain in the valley below and talked in whispers. Smith asking questions about Korea and its customs and Woo was intrigued by a place called Georgia. At a little past eleven, Woo felt the urge to relieve himself. Crawling out of the fox-hole, he moved off into the darkness, telling Smith that he wouldn't be gone long.

Alone now, the anxious Smith peered out across the craters of the moonlike landscape below, his eyes steadily moving along the rows of silvery stumps. Suddenly, his heart skipped a beat as two fleeting figures dashed across the valley floor and vanished into the silver-gray forest of tree stumps directly below his position. For several minutes he watched the area where the figures had disappeared, but saw nothing. He had only observed them for a few seconds, but was certain his eyes were not playing tricks on him. There was someone down there.

Grabbing the direct land-line phone connected to Lieutenant Bressler's command post, Smith reported the sighting. Was he certain he saw something? asked the command post. Affirmative, replied Smith. He had seen two men running at a crouch, both carrying rifles. Smith's report was the first alert Baker Company received of the coming attack.

Bressler immediately notified Lieutenant Patterson of the sighting and requested that artillery fire illumination rounds over the outpost for confirmation.

At Listening Post 21, Private Smith's heart was pounding a mile a second. Where was Private Lee Woo? Why wasn't he back yet? From somewhere behind him, Smith heard the distant firing of artillery.

Within seconds illumination rounds were exploding high over his head, lighting up the outpost and the terrain around it. What the young private saw in the eerie yellow glow of that light nearly took his breath away. The entire valley floor and the base of the ridge below were covered with Chinese soldiers—hundreds of them. They were scrambling across the barren, crater-pocked landscape like some giant colony of ants. And they were all headed for their anthill—Outpost Dale.

Smith grabbed his phone again and attempted to contact Lieutenant Bressler. The line was dead. At that same moment, at the far end of the ridge, Listening Post 17 opened fire, but they were far too late. Smith could clearly see the muzzle flashes of their weapons reflecting off the enemies' uniforms moments before they were overrun. The perimeter machine guns opened up from the ridge line above him. Smith watched the red tracers from the machine guns reach out like lethal fingers and tear into the onrushing ant colony, but it did little to stop them. They kept coming up the hill at a steady pace.

Grabbing his rifle, Smith jumped out of his foxhole and called out, "Woo! Woo! Where are you? There was no reply. Suddenly, bullets began to zing past Smith's head as others kicked up the dirt and rock around him. It was time to abandon the listening post. Running up the hill, he leaped into the relative safety of the perimeter trench and raced toward the command bunker.

Gunfire was erupting all over the hill. Smith located the command post and burst into the small room. Lieutenant Bressler was on the radio requesting artillery fire. Seeing Smith, he paused and waited for his report. Nearly out of breath and a little shaken by the sudden rush of events, Smith nervously informed his commander that hundreds of Chinese were moving up the hill and that most if not all of the listening posts had been overrun.

Lieutenant Bressler, himself only twenty-four years old, made a lasting impression on young Smith in those few minutes. The young officer's expression never changed. There were no signs of panic; on the contrary, Bressler demonstrated the calmness one would expect from a veteran twice his years. This show of confidence helped ease the anxiety in Private Smith. In a clear and unwavering voice, Bressler told Smith to find the platoon sergeant and to have him reinforce the east and west ends of the trench line and then start drawing the platoon back toward the command post. Did the young private understand? asked Bressler.

Smith nodded, saluted, then raced back out into the trench. Exploding artillery, grenades, and Chinese mortar rounds were now adding to the chaos of the battle that in some places was going hand-to-hand. All up and down the line, Smith heard the agonizing cry, "Medic! Medic!"

Rounding a cut in the trench, Smith ran head-on into three Chinese soldiers, knocking down two of them. In a wild shooting spree that lasted less than ten seconds, Smith was wounded in the arm and the three Chinese were killed.

Shaken, but determined not to be deterred from his mission, Smith crawled over the dead men and continued his run for the platoon sergeant's bunker. By the time he arrived, it was too late. The platoon sergeant and two other men from Baker Company were lying dead near the doorway of the bunker. The bodies of ten Chinese were piled around them.

Someone down the line yelled, "They're in the trenches!" This was old news to the private from Georgia.

Smith decided he had better return to the command post and advise the lieutenant that the platoon sergeant was dead. Reversing his direction, he again raced down the trench, yelling to those that could still hear him to fall back on the command post. They were going to make their stand there.

Less than fifty yards from the post, Smith came to a dead stop. Several Chinese grenades came rolling down the slope and landed in the trench directly in front of him. In desperation, the boy threw his body out of the trench and tumbled a short distance down the hill. Seconds later the trench was rocked by a series of deafening explosions.

Smith lay exhausted. His breathing coming in short, labored gasps, and he became painfully aware of the bullet hole through his arm. He suddenly realized he'd lost his rifle in the roll down the hill. Raising his head, he tried to locate the weapon in the flashes of artillery and mortar fire. At the instant Smith saw the rifle, something grabbed his left leg. With his heart in his throat, Smith turned his head and looked back. Private Lee Chang Woo had a hold of his leg. The right side of the Korean's shirt was a bloody mess and there was a nasty gash along the left side of his neck, as if someone had tried to cut his throat.

Relieved that it was not the enemy, Smith pivoted on his stomach and pulled the wounded South Korean into a nearby shell crater. Tearing open the boy's shirt, Smith noticed a small crucifix hanging from a thin leather thong around Woo's neck. It surprised Smith. He hadn't really thought much about

Koreans believing in God or religion. Moving the small cross aside, Smith went to work on Woo. There was a gash that started at the chest and sliced to a gaping hole just below the armpit. He removed a compress from Woo's aid packet, pressed it over the hole, and told Woo to hold it in place. Smith placed the bandage from his own aid packet firmly against the neck wound to stop the bleeding. All the while he was whispering, "Hang in there, Woo, you're going to make it, buddy. Just hang on."

Lee Woo nodded in obvious pain, and while Smith worked, told him what had happened. Within minutes of leaving the foxhole he had been grabbed by two men who had seemed to come up out of the ground. In a sudden move one of them had his hand over Woo's mouth so that he could not shout a warning. The other man had driven a knife into his chest, but the blade had glanced off and gone sideways. Next there had been a burning sensation along the left side of his neck, and he had passed out. The Chinese had apparently taken his weapon and left him for dead. When he awoke, the battle was going on. He had been clawing his way slowly up the hill when Smith had suddenly come rolling down the hill and stopped only a few feet from him.

When Smith had finished tending the wounds and slumped back against the slope of the crater, Lee Woo asked, "Are we winning or losing?"

"I don't know," replied Smith. "The platoon sergeant's dead and a lot of our guys are hurt. The Chinese are in the trenches and a few minutes ago I saw the command post take a direct hit."

"The lieutenant?" asked Woo.

Smith shook his head. "Don't know who's runnin' the show. All I do know is we're out here with Chinese everywhere and neither one of us has a weapon. If they stumble onto us, we've had it.''

Forcing a slight smile through his pain, Woo clutched his small cross and answered, ''There is only one who can say when it shall be our time. And after all we have been through tonight, I do not believe He intends for us to die now.''

Whether from exhaustion, fear, or frustration, Smith wasn't sure which, he answered bitterly, ''Yeah! Right! The big guy upstairs is just going to let 'em chew us up a little at a time before they finish us off. Is that it?''

Private Woo did not reply.

''Where'd you get that cross anyway?'' asked Smith.

''Missionary school. Long ago,'' said Woo. ''They taught us that if one believed strongly in his heart, then one would earn the protection of the warriors of the Lord. Do you believe, Joe Smith?''

Smith looked away for a moment. How ironic, he thought. He had come thousands of miles to fight in a war he knew little about, had almost been killed twice tonight, and was now being reminded by a South Korean soldier of what his mother and his church had told him for years—always to put his faith in God.

''Yes, I believe, Woo. But it's been a long time.''

''Does not matter, Smith. As long as one believes, there is hope,'' said Woo with a smile.

The little South Korean was about to recite a prayer when Smith suddenly dropped down beside him and placed his hand over Woo's mouth. Emerging from the smoke and dust to their right was a group of Communist Chinese soldiers. Their direction of movement would bring them straight to the crater in which Smith and Woo were now hidden. Smith looked at Woo. The man's eyes were closed. "Chinese—lots of 'em coming this way," whispered Smith.

The man from Georgia had never felt so totally helpless. They were both wounded. They had no weapons. And they couldn't run. What were they going to do? Smith could feel the panic rising within him. He looked up over the rim. The Chinese had not changed direction. They would be at the hole within minutes.

Suddenly Smith heard a whispered phrase come from behind him. "Do not fear, for thy host are with thee."

Looking back at Woo, Smith saw the man's eyes were still closed. For a moment he thought the Korean soldier was dead. Slowly he ran the phrase through his mind. "Do not fear, for thy host are with thee." Almost instantly an idea came to Smith.

Removing the bandage from Woo's neck, he purposely reopened the wound. Pulling the tourniquet from his own arm, he forced a small pool of blood into his hand and smeared it over the left side of his own face, whispering, "We've got to play dead, Woo. It's our only chance."

Sliding down slightly, Smith laid the upper part of his body across Woo's legs, assuring that the blood-smeared part of his face was clearly visible to anyone looking down into the hole.

The sound of the enemies' boots moving along the rock-strewn slope grew more distinct as they neared the crater. In those few minutes, Joseph Smith recalled every prayer he had ever heard in his short twenty years on the earth.

Suddenly, they were there. Smith's heart nearly

stopped as he felt dirt and rocks from the edge of the crater trickle down against his outstretched leg. He knew the enemy soldiers were standing directly over them and staring down at their bodies. There was a quick exchange of words among the Chinese. Then the sound of a bolt going back and locking into place. Every muscle in Smith's body tensed as he waited for the hail of machine gun bullets he knew were about to rip through his body.

He heard the trigger click and the bolt go forward, but nothing happened. Smith didn't know a word of Chinese, but could tell by the shooter's tone of voice that the weapon had misfired. There were a few laughs, then from the other side of the crater he heard a bolt slide back. The trigger clicked and the bolt went forward. Again nothing happened. There were more laughs, then a third bolt went back. Smith knew their luck had ran out. Two misfires were nothing short of a miracle in itself, but three would be impossible. Yet this weapon also misfired.

There was an angry exchange of words, then Smith heard the sounds of the boots moving across the rocks again. This time they were going away from the crater. Waiting a few minutes, Smith dared to move his head ever so slightly and opened one eye just enough to see that there was no one standing around the crater. The Chinese soldiers were gone.

Easing himself up to the edge of the crater, Smith peered out across the slope. There was no one there. The battle had shifted from Outpost Dale and was now being fought on another hill to the northeast.

Smith, physically and mentally exhausted, slid back down beside Lee Woo. The South Korean had a grin on his face and was clutching his small crucifix.

"I just knew they were going to shoot us to pieces," said Smith.

"They were," answered Woo. "But their guns would not work."

"Yeah. Misfire, I guess."

"One, maybe. Two, not impossible. But three? I do not think so," said Woo. "You must believe very much, Smith."

Smith now smiled, "Yes, I do. But I have to admit, I was pretty rattled there for a minute until you said that little prayer of yours."

Lee Woo looked at the Georgian strangely for a moment, then at his cross.

"What's wrong?" asked Smith.

Lee Woo then informed his friend that when Smith had placed his hand over his mouth, Woo had lost consciousness for a short time. He remembered nothing until he came to and heard the voices of the Chinese standing over them. Smith was stunned. "Then how ... Who ... Oh, come on now, Woo. You telling me you didn't say, 'Do not fear, for thy host are with thee'?"

Lee Woo shook his head slightly from side to side. "No, my friend. I did not."

A confused Smith muttered, "Then who ... ?"

Lee Woo only grinned and replied, "The warriors of the Lord do not have to be seen to be heard by true believers."

Following the battle at Outpost Dale, Private Lee Chang Woo was evacuated to a hospital in Seoul where doctors worked to reverse the damage to his right arm. Severe nerve damage however, left the arm partially paralyzed, and Woo was discharged from the South Korean army six months later. He continued to work for the U.S. army as an interpreter for the remainder of the Korean war. In appreciation of his loyal service, Lee Woo and his family were brought to the United States, where they received their American citizenship in 1956.

Lee Chang Woo went on to become a successful businessman with an electronics firm in Los Angeles. He is now retired, and he and his wife enjoy tending their flower gardens and are active in their local church. Interestingly enough, Lee Woo presented his cross to his son, who served as a Marine in Vietnam. When the chopper in which the boy was riding went down, Woo's son was the only survivor.

Joseph Smith also survived the Korean war. He returned home to Georgia only long enough to marry his hometown sweetheart. Finding the army to his liking, he remained in the service until he retired in 1975. Now sixty years old and an avid golfer, he still enjoys telling the story of his talk with the angels and of the great experience he had one night in 1953 on the slope of a war-torn hill, where a Korean soldier renewed his faith in God.

## 21

# *Angels at Four O'clock*

*Four angels to my bed.*
*Four angels round my head,*
*One to watch, and one to pray,*
*And two to bear my soul away.*

—THOMAS ADY, "A Candle in the Dark"

TWENTY-SIX-YEAR-OLD SERGEANT LARRY REYNOLDS didn't remember being hit. One minute he had been firing on a swarm of screaming North Koreans charging up a hill to overrun his company's position. He remembered the terrible sound of the long, whining notes of blowing bugles in the background that seemed to drive the attackers into a frenzy, like wild-eyed sharks converging on a bleeding man.

Now he lay at the feet of three North Koreans. Their bayoneted rifles pressed painfully against his chest and throat. He could still hear shooting, but not as loud now. Only random shots, or quick, short bursts from machine guns. What Sergeant Reynolds didn't know was that the shots he heard around him were the North Koreans shooting the American wounded deemed too seriously hurt or too bothersome to be taken prisoner.

As a small trickle of blood began to leak from the tip of the bayonet at his throat, Reynolds saw another North Korean approach. Judging from the insignia on his epaulets, the man was an officer. He knelt down next to the sergeant, jerked the watch off the American's wrist, and placed it in his shirt pocket. He then ripped the sergeant's shirt open to examine his wound. Reynolds had been lucky. It was a straight-through shot that had entered above the fourth rib of his right side, gone around the bone, and exited in the back. Painful, but not deadly.

Reynolds was roughly pulled to his feet. One of the bayonets poked at his back, encouraging him to start moving. A light rain began to fall as he was prodded forward to join other American prisoners being held at the base of the hill. He recognized a few of the POWs. Seeing his friend Corporal Thomas Beehan covered in blood and weaving uneasily on his feet, Reynolds went over to him. "Hang on, kid. We'll get you some help pretty soon."

The sergeant's words of encouragement brought the instant response of a Communist rifle butt into the middle of his back, the blow sending the wounded man to his knees.

"No talking!" shouted a short Korean guard.

Reynolds managed to regain his feet, silently uttering a string of curses under his breath. If only he had a rifle or a knife, he thought, things would be a lot different. But he didn't. He was now a prisoner of war. To the professional soldier that was a fate worse than death. His survival now depended on the whims of his captors, and if this early greeting was any sign of the North Koreans' concern over the rules of the Geneva Convention, Sergeant Reynolds and his fellow prisoners were at the doorway leading to a trip into hell itself.

After the prisoners stood in the rain for nearly an hour, the Korean officer who had relieved Reynolds of his watch came walking down the mountain with his men. There were no other Americans with them. Of the 142 men of Reynolds's company, only forty-four were still alive. Bleeding and battered, the prisoners began the slow, agonizing walk toward the enemies' homeland.

North Korea is a land of mountains, not rolling hills or gentle valleys, but rather harsh, unyielding ground of sharp-pointed rocks covered with a thin layer of soil. The prisoners' boots, worn from long use and weather, afforded little protection from the jagged rocks. All along the line, prisoners stumbled on the sharp stones, or twisted ankles and fell. Each stumble earned the unfortunate POW a jab from a bayonet.

Soon, more prisoners joined Reynolds's group. Some of them had been stripped to the waist. They were practically freezing, their lips turning blue at the edges. All were exhausted, battle-weary, with a look of shock and disbelief on their faces. Each mile of the way, the column grew in size and in suffering. Soon, those weakened from the weather conditions and their wounds began to fall out, unable to go another step. When a POW fell, a guard would step over him, ram a bayonet through his neck, and leave him to bleed to death.

One of the prisoners was a medic. He still wore

the Red Cross armband. When a man near him was bayoneted, the medic instinctively dropped out of line to stop the flow of blood. Another guard stepped up, and while the medic was kneeling, shot him through the head.

The shot brought an officer storming up the column. He shouted and waved his arms in a rage. He picked up the empty cartridge from the ground and shook it in the guard's face. It was clear that he was reprimanding the guard for wasting ammunition. As if to emphasize how killing should be done, the officer yanked a prisoner out of the line. Grabbing the guard's rifle, he drove his bayonet through the captive's neck. This was more than the prisoners could stand. They broke ranks and surged forward toward the officer. Rifle fire erupted. Unarmed men fell. North Koreans beat at their captives with their rifle butts. Once order had been reestablished, the officer upon which the prisoners had vented their rage lay on the ground, an American trench knife sticking from his throat.

Enraged by the sight of their dead officer and the fact that someone had been carrying a concealed weapon, the guards forced everyone to strip naked in the freezing rain. The guards pillaged through the mound of worn and bloody clothes, stealing wallets, money, rings, watches, and even pens. What undergarments remained, the shivering prisoners put back on their freezing wet bodies. Night came, and with it sleet and hail. The POWs huddled together for warmth and a sense of protection. The long, cold night seemed to last an eternity.

As morning came, many of the men did not respond to the bayonet prodding. They were dead. To make sure, the guards moved among the prone and huddled figures, stabbing each of them three or four times with their bayonets. When the line began to move again, only the dead remained behind. Reynolds consoled himself—at least he wasn't dead. Yet neither was he totally alive. His feet were on the verge of freezing and began to swell.

After four torturous days and nights, more fallen men, more bloodshed, the nightmare march finally ended inside the walls of a North Korean prison. The small, dungeon-type cells lined either side of a narrow passageway. Two men were forced into each of these small spaces and the iron-bar doors locked behind them. Talking was forbidden. To be caught talking meant being pulled from your cell and beaten senseless.

As cold and miserable as it was in that horrid place, Sergeant Reynolds was grateful finally to be in a place where he could get off his feet. His ankles had swollen and both feet had bulged to an enormous size. The skin was cracking and beginning to fester. He knew what it was—trench rot. Without medication and a way to keep his feet dry, there was no hope of a cure. Soon, his condition had become so bad that Reynolds could no longer walk. He had to crawl if he needed to move about.

Sharing this damp hole of iniquity with Reynolds was a fighter pilot whose plane had been shot down only hours before Reynolds had been captured. His first name was Shannon, a twenty-four-year old from Macon, Georgia. Last names and rank meant nothing in that place. Simply staying alive was all that mattered. To do that, each man would have to have the support of the other, the stronger aiding the weaker as best he could.

The guards came by each cell and tossed a single

bucket onto the floor. This would be their toilet. Each morning at daylight, the cells were opened one at a time and a single prisoner was allowed to take the bucket above ground to empty it into an open sewer, then returned to his cell. Since Reynolds could not walk, the task fell to Shannon.

Following his first trip to the sewer and back, Reynolds asked Shannon in a whisper, "What's it like up there?"

Shannon, his voice barely audible, replied, "Not much. There are lots of other underground barracks. I saw other men dumping their buckets farther down the line."

"Is there a wall around this building?"

"No, just another building. The wall is farther away."

A guard approached and the two men fell silent.

Reynolds and Shannon had been placed in an end cell. This location had good points and bad points. One good point was that there was no through traffic and the poorly supervised guards seldom bothered to walk the entire length of the corridor. Both a good point and a bad point was the existence of a small opening at the top of their cell where a brick had been knocked out to provide an air vent. This caused a constant draft of cold air to circulate about the cell, which did little to help Reynolds's foot problem. However, occasionally a small amount of sunlight would creep through, lessening the gloom of their small place of existence.

Soon the days began to merge into one another and time was a forgotten thing. Occasionally they heard the sounds of a cell being opened and a man being removed for interrogation or for burial. Whispering became an art. The men found that if words were murmured at just the right pitch they could be heard only by other inmates in the immediate area. An entire alphabet of sign language was invented and passed along from cell to cell. By using this ingenious system, the prisoners were able to pass messages throughout the cellblock.

Any real news from the outside was infrequent, but rumors were constant. Some prisoners were detailed to serve their one meal a day, which usually consisted of fishheads and moldy rice. As these servers ladled the meals into prisoners' bowls they would whisper the latest news. "MacArthur . . . He's marching north. Big push on. Ought to be here in a couple of days?"

"You mean we'll be free in a few days?"

"Yeah, sure. You know MacArthur, he won't forget us. We'll be out of here soon."

Of course, such rumors only added momentary hope. As the days came and went, disappointment replaced hope, but just as quickly another rumor would soon spread.

On one particularly cold day, Shannon tore part of his shirt in strips and wrapped them around Reynolds's painful feet.

"Morale is terrible," he whispered. "We're all losing hope. You can feel it spreading down the hallway like the plague. The men need something to hold on to. Some kind of hope."

"Yeah, but what?" replied Reynolds, in obvious pain.

"I don't know. If only we could have prayer sessions. Let them hear some words of hope or promise."

Reynolds quickly shook his head. "No way. You saw what happened to Corporal North."

A few days earlier, Corporal Alvin North had shocked everyone on the cellblock by loudly and clearly reciting the Lord's Prayer. Before he could finish, five guards jerked him from his cell and beat him with clubs and a bullwhip, almost killing him.

"Besides," said Reynolds, "God has abandoned this place. Relinquished it to the devil as his own private hell."

"Don't say that, Sarge!" said Shannon, gripping the sergeant's hand tightly. "You know you don't mean it."

"Oh, yeah!" barked Reynolds, tears appearing in his painridden eyes. "Well, you figure we're going to get any help in this hellhole?"

Shannon reached up and cradled his comrade's tearstained face against his shoulder and softly whispered, " 'I will lift up my mine eyes unto the hills, from whence cometh my help. My help cometh from the Lord . . .' "

Reynolds, the hard-core veteran, broke down and wept. Shannon held him until the sergeant had let it all out, then gently laid Reynolds back on the straw mat that served as a bed, allowing him to drift off to sleep.

The next morning when Shannon returned from dumping their bucket of waste, Reynolds held out his hand and thanked the pilot for his words of comfort the previous night. "No need for thanks, Sarge."

"Were you a preacher or something before you came in?" asked Reynolds.

"No, I just read the Bible a lot. I believe that there is a reason for everything that happens in this world. I also believe that each of us is blessed with a guardian angel to watch over us."

"Well you'd be hard-pressed to convince Corporal

North of that right now, or those guys we left back on that road,'' said Reynolds with a hint of doubt in his voice.

''No, not really,'' answered Shannon calmly. ''From the moment we are born, our destiny has already been preplanned. How we prepare ourselves along the way is up to each of us. North was beaten, true, but for what reason? Because he acknowledged the words of God. But he didn't die, did he?''

Reynolds thought about that for a moment. ''But what about the men who did die?''

''It was their destiny. They had reached a time and place where their lives were meant to come to an end. How they conducted their lives up to that time will be judged another day. Just as I am here with you and the others right now. I am confident that this is where I was destined to be at this moment in my life. For what reason I do not know. But as long as I believe, I know that reason will be shown to me one day.''

Reynolds stared a long time at the pilot he'd never met before. What a strong faith the man had. If only his were as strong.

Shannon leaned against the wall, his eyes traveling up to the small opening at the top of their cell through which a small beam of sunlight had slowly entered. A smile suddenly crossed his face as an idea came to him. Moving to the wall, he reached up on tiptoes for the hole. It was just out of reach. There was no furniture in the cell, nothing he could stand on.

''What are you doing?'' asked Reynolds.

''If I could see out that hole, maybe we could find out what's going on around us.''

''Good idea,'' replied the sergeant. Crawling over

to the wall, he arched his back and told Shannon to
step up. Maybe he could get high enough to see out.

Both men were weak from their lack of proper
food, but managed to accomplish the task after a few
minutes. The prisoner across from them watched for
the approach of any guards and would warn them if
he saw anything. Shannon's weight at first almost
drove Reynolds to the floor, but they managed the
maneuver and Shannon was soon peering out the
small opening. "What do you see?" whispered
Reynolds.

Shannon was silent for a long moment, then whispered, "One of our jets, way off in the distance. He
just shot down two Korean Migs. I can see them
going down."

After a few moments, Reynolds began to wobble.
Shannon lost his balance and fell to the floor. The
two men lay staring at each other like two excited
children. "Two Migs ... hot damn," whispered
Reynolds. Dragging himself across the filthy floor to
the bars of their cell, he passed the news on to the
man across from him, who in turn passed it along
the cellblock. "One of our jets downed two Migs."
It was great news. Morale instantly improved in the
cellblock.

Each day around noon, Shannon would repeat the
action. Some days there was nothing to report or the
weather was too bad to see anything. Then one day,
Shannon reported seeing a flight of American fighters
attacking an enemy column marching across a distant
mountain. The column had been totally wiped out by
the jets. This brought an upsurge in spirits for
everyone.

Each day the prisoners waited for Shannon's reports. They lived for the daily accounts as if they

were hot news bulletins, fresh off the press. They had Shannon describe the terrain.

"There's a mountain off in the distance," he told them. A main road runs along its side. That's where the jets caught the troops in the open. It was a real slaughter. There's a train tunnel just to the right of the road about a quarter mile away."

Every man in the cellblock had a vivid picture in his mind of the scene Shannon described to them. The meal servers began to give Shannon an extra ladle of food. They wanted to assure that he kept up his strength. The guards began to notice an upsurge in the spirits of their captives, but they could never figure it out. The secret of the peephole was preserved.

Eventually new prisoners were brought in. They provided fresh news. MacArthur had launched an all-out invasion. South Korean troops, backed by American forces, were slicing a path through North Korea. Even paratroopers were being used for the operation.

Shannon's observations through the peephole to the world confirmed these rumors. One day he saw an American gunship catch a supply train in its sights just as it reached the tunnel. The whole thing had exploded, destroying both the train and the tunnel. This was great news. On another day, he saw paratroopers floating down beyond the mountain. But they hadn't come to rescue the POWs. Maybe soon.

Then one day the prisoners didn't need Shannon's eyes. They could hear the action themselves. It was the sound of aerial combat, and it was directly over the prison. Something was definitely going on, for even their guards had rushed outside to join in the action. When they returned, their anger was apparent.

They took it out on the hapless prisoners, beating some almost to death.

Two days later, the rescue began. American forces could be heard in the area. Yes, Shannon could see them on the mountainside. They were GIs and they were advancing. The guards again left the cellblock. "What do you see, Shannon?" asked Reynolds, his voice filled with excitement. What is it?" shouted the others, no longer fearful now that the guards were gone.

There was a long moment of silence before Shannon answered softly, "Angels at four o'clock . . . and they're coming this way. I can see them clearly."

"Jets! More jets!" shouted someone. "They're here. What are we waiting for?" Excitement gripped the entire cellblock. The prisoners rioted. Hidden makeshift keys appeared and doors magically opened. Men rushed for the exits. Shannon stepped to the floor. There was a strange look on his face, almost peaceful. Reynolds slapped his leg, "Go for it, kid! Get out of here! Don't worry about me. I'll be out soon enough. Go on."

Shannon nodded and looked toward the door, as if he saw something there. Stepping out of the cell, Shannon turned to the sergeant. "Good-bye, Sergeant Reynolds. It would seem our help has cometh as promised. God be with you."

Shannon made it as far as the exit before the guards rushed back into the building. In a flurry of gunfire, many of the unarmed men were shot down, Shannon among them. In desperation, Reynolds crawled out of the cell on his knees and pulled the mortally wounded pilot back into their cell. This act prevented a guard from bayoneting the wounded man.

Holding Shannon in his lap, Reynolds rocked him gently as a mother would a sick child. There were tears in his eyes, for he was helpless to do anything to save his friend. All he could do was try to comfort him until the end came.

"Easy, boy," whispered the sergeant. "The pain will be gone soon."

Shannon opened his eyes. There was no pain in his eyes as he uttered, "I was shown . . . the reason, Sarge. I know why now . . . There were . . . angels . . . angels at four . . . o'clock. They . . . they smiled and beckoned to me . . . 'I will lift up . . . mine eyes . . . unto the hills . . .' " Shannon's eyes closed and he died.

Sobbing openly, Reynolds held him and whispered, " 'I will lift up mine eyes unto the hills, from whence cometh my help. My help cometh from the Lord . . .' "

The next morning American troops overran the POW camp and liberated the captives. Leaning against a wall with Shannon's head still in his lap, Reynolds stared up blankly at two stretcher bearers who entered his cell. They gently removed Shannon's body, then came back for Reynolds. "Come on, Sarge! We're here to take you to the biggest damn dinner you ever saw."

As they started to put him on the stretcher, Reynolds cried out, "Wait!" Can you do me a favor?"

"Sure, Sarge. You've earned it. What d' you need?"

"Lift me up and let me look out though that hole up there."

The two men exchanged glances, then shrugged. What the heck. If that was what he wanted, so be it. Because he was hardly more than skin and bones by now, it took, little effort to hoist Reynolds up on the shoulders of one of the men. "Well, take a good look, Sarge, if that's what you want."

Leaning forward, Reynolds brought his face to the hole and stared through the small opening . . . straight into the brick wall of the building next door. Shannon had discovered his purpose for being there. That purpose had been to provide the most precious gift he could at the time: the gift of hope.

# THE
# VIETNAM WAR

WITHOUT A DOUBT, EACH GENERATION THAT HAS EN-
dured the horrors of war would argue that the war
in which they participated was more hellish than any
other before that time.

I heartily agree. Having spent three tours of duty
in the Republic of Vietnam, I can honestly say that
those of us who fought there will always remember
that place as a true hell on earth.

There were two enemies in Vietnam. One was the
country itself, with its sweltering heat, monsoon
rains, and dense jungle that seems to reach out and
grab you, threatening to swallow you whole into its
vastness at the first sign of weakness.

The other was the military enemy, as elusive in
the cities and villages as they were in the terrain of
the jungles they knew so well. There were no safe
havens in Vietnam. A person eating breakfast in a
hotel restaurant could die as easily as a grunt on
patrol. It was a different war than my father had

known in World War II. The enemy in Vietnam came in all sizes, ages, genders, and uniforms, from the khaki of the NVA regular to the black pajamas of the Vietcong, from the ragged clothes of a small boy with a shoeshine box to the robes of a supposed holy monk. The enemy had only two rules: to fight to the death, and to win. Unfortunately, our rules included the first, but not the second.

The Vietnam war officially lasted for ten years. In that time over fifty-five thousand American soldiers made the ultimate sacrifice. As in wars throughout time, there were the miraculous and the unexplainable. The following are but a few such stories. I am certain many more have yet to be told. The next story is my own. At the time it happened, I considered it nothing more than just luck, but after working on this book, I realize there was much more to it than that. After reading it, see if you don't agree. Some things simply cannot be explained ... or can they?

## 22

# The Hammer and the Cross

*Angels, where e'er we go,*
*Attend our steps whate'er betide.*
*With watchful care their charge attend*
*And evil turn aside.*

IT WAS APRIL 1969. THE EFFECTS OF THE TET OFFENsive of late 1968 were still being felt throughout the country. The American press was having a field day hammering General William Westmoreland and the American officers in charge of running the war in Vietnam. College kids across the nation were protesting and asking some very pointed questions that leaders were having a difficult time answering.

Amid all this controversy, I found myself in the sixth month of my assignment with a Special Forces recon unit working out of the northern province of Da Nang. We were a top-secret organization that conducted classified operations north of the demilitarized zone, and across the borders into Laos and

Cambodia. It was a highly dangerous assignment, and the unit took only volunteers for its operations.

I had been fortunate enough to be assigned to a team that included two highly respected and well-regarded veterans: Sergeant First Class John Dodds and Sergeant Mike "Buck" Buchannan. Both men had completed a previous tour of Vietnam and returned for a second. Within three months they had taught me all the ins and outs of surviving in Vietnam, or at least the things that had worked for them. And since both of these men had run over twenty missions and had not been awarded a free trip home in a plastic bag, I figured they knew what they were talking about.

In February 1969 John's luck ran out. Having conducted a recon in the DMZ, we were awaiting the arrival of our extraction helicopters when a squad of NVA stumbled onto us. In a running gun battle, John was hit in both legs by automatic weapons fire and dropped like a wet bag of cement. Luckily, our support aircraft were over us a few minutes later and the NVA chose to split rather than deal with massive amounts of napalm and five-hundred-pound bombs. We got John loaded and out of there. He was back in the States a week later.

While waiting for a replacement for John, Buck and I occupied our time by working with an order of French nuns who ran a Vietnamese orphanage down the road from our compound.

The sisters had converted an old French fort into a relatively comfortable home for kids ranging in age from six months to sixteen years. Buck and I would spend all our free time repairing leaking roofs, building makeshift beds from discarded wooden crates, and traveling to other Special Forces camps to raise donations for the sisters. It seemed that there was never enough money. When we began there were only thirty-five children. Within a month that number had grown to one hundred and fifty, and Buck and I were determined to help each and every one of them. It was a labor of love that was most appreciated by the sisters.

One day, we were delivering some supplies we had "liberated" in that unique fashion of which Green Berets were often accused in Vietnam. (We will not discuss that further, except to say that often the end justifies the means.) Anyway, that morning the sisters presented us with two gold crosses on solid gold chains. At first we scolded them for spending their much-needed funds on things for us and felt that we could not accept such expensive gifts from them. But we saw the hurt expressions on their faces, and after further encouragement by the mother superior, we reluctantly accepted the gifts. After unloading the supplies, we thanked them again and returned to our base.

The following morning we were notified to report to the operations center, which was overwhelmed with recon mission requests from Saigon. Even though we still did not have a replacement for Dodds, the team would have to take one of the missions. We shrugged and replied, "No sweat."

The mission was a photo intelligence sweep of the Ho Chi Minh Trail in the northwestern corner of the DMZ. Saigon also wanted a prisoner if possible.

The night before we were to be inserted into the target area, Buck took off his cross and placed it in a personnel items bag that would be left behind. I took mine off and looked at it for a long moment, feeling a sense of pride in what it meant and why I had received it. Rubbing it, I remembered what one of the sisters had said: "Now you will have God with you wherever you go, to watch over you and protect you."

When I placed the cross back around my neck, Buck seemed surprised. We never wore jewelry on operations. Sunlight could reflect off a ring or chain and give away your position. I assured Buck that I would keep my shirt buttoned high enough so that neither the cross nor the chain would show. He still didn't think much of the idea, but let it go at that.

The following day we went into the target area. By mid-afternoon we had reached a good position from which to photograph the traffic along one branch of the Ho Chi Minh Trail. We didn't have to wait long for something to photograph. Adjusting the telescoping lens, Buck began to take pictures of over two hundred NVA regulars moving down the trail to the south. One hour later, we had another hundred, half of whom were pushing bicycles loaded with bags of rice and ammunition strapped across the handlebars. They too were moving toward the south. The stream of traffic continued on and off all afternoon. Each time we took pictures and waited for a smaller group of NVA to pass that would offer us the opportunity to grab a prisoner and get out of there. By nightfall, we moved back, deep into the jungle, and rested for the night. We would try again at first light the next morning.

As predawn gray broke along the horizon we moved back into position. Our early rising soon proved beneficial. We had been in position less than five minutes when six NVA came around a bend in the trail, walking as nonchalantly as if they were on a Sunday stroll, their rifles held across their shoulders and their hands dangling over the stock and barrel. I signaled Buck that I would take down the lead man; he would be our prisoner. Buck and the others would take out the other five.

The weapons of choice for POW snatches were rifles with silencers and a .38-caliber pistol, also silenced. I would hit the lead man in both kneecaps to drop him while Buck and the team would kill the other five with single shots to the head. The key to the operation was silence; the sound of gunfire always drew a crowd. At least that was the well-rehearsed plan that we had come up with back at the base. But few plans ever work as well as they do in rehearsal. This one was to be no exception.

Taking a deep breath, I sighted in on the lead man's right knee. I couldn't help noticing that he was big for a Vietnamese. Buck readied the team. Their rifles sighted in on the heads of the other five soldiers as they approached. I began counting to myself. One . . . two . . . took up the slack in the trigger . . . three. I fired. The pistol jumped in my hand and the lead man grunted as the bullet spun him around and to the ground. At the same instant, the others fired and I saw four of the five fall instantly. The fifth had not been hit in the head, but rather in the neck. Before a second shot could be made, the man squeezed off a burst from his AK-47. The thundering roar of the gunfire echoed through the jungle. At the time it seem to be the loudest thing I'd ever heard.

Breaking from cover, I rushed toward the wounded NVA I had shot. He had dropped his rifle when he fell and was now crawling in a desperate effort to reach it. Buck and the team hurried out to finish off the others and move the bodies away from the trail.

Reaching my man just as his hand touched the

rifle, I kicked it away. In that instant, the NVA swung his good leg around and swept my feet out from under me. I hit the ground hard, momentarily knocking the wind out of me. Before I could react, the NVA was on top of me, his hands grabbing for the pistol I still held in my left hand. Raising my leg, I kicked the man to the side and we rolled over and over until we tumbled into a small ditch beside the trail. Struggling with all my might, I forced the man to the side and tried to bring the pistol down on his head to break his grip on my throat, but he was as hardheaded as he was tough.

As we battled in the ditch, I heard the sound of gunfire again. Buck and the team were engaged in a firefight with a squad of NVA who had come to investigate the earlier shooting. If I was going to survive the battle with this NVA I was going to have to do it myself. Buck and the others were too busy to help me now.

A sudden pain shot through my right arm and I realized that the man had produced a knife from somewhere and driven it deep into my right shoulder, narrowly missing my chest. The knife came up again and I blocked it, but not before it cut a gash above my left eye. My pistol had been knocked loose and was lying beside us. The NVA brought the knife up again. This time I was ready. Bringing my head up as hard as I could, I head-butted the man right between the eyes. He screamed and grabbed for his eyes. As he did, I knocked the knife away and rolled him off me, while trying to catch my breath.

In that instant, the NVA grabbed for the pistol. It was a good grab. He held the gun in both hands. Desperately, I reached out and gripped his wrists. The gun was between us. With his thumb, he managed to cock the pistol. From my angle and position in the ditch, it was all I could do to hold on to his hands. Slowly, he leaned forward with all his weight, struggling to bring the pistol up under my chin. Blood ran down into my eye from the gash, blurring my vision. My breathing was heavy. This man was incredibly strong for a Vietnamese.

As we struggled, he managed to twist the gun to the side and force it up under the right side of my chin. I saw his finger going toward the trigger. In that instant, I realized I was about to die. In a cry of both fear and frustration, I cried out, "Oh, God! Please help me!"

My plea did not interest the NVA soldier as he increased his pressure on the pistol. Although it was not directly under my chin, he was satisfied with the gun's position. The shot might not kill me, but it would blow half my face away, then he could finish the job.

I could see in his eyes that he was about to fire. I tensed as I felt his hand jerk the trigger and waited for my face to come apart. But there was only a click. The weapon had not fired. This unexpected event momentarily stunned my enemy. He looked down at the gun in disbelief. When he did, I brought my knee up as hard as I could. The blow caught him square in the middle of the back and sent him flying over my head. In one desperate move I grabbed his knife. The thought of taking a prisoner was no longer relevant to me. With all my might, I brought the knife down into the center of the man's chest, killing him instantly.

Exhausted, I slumped back against the ditch. My hands were trembling as I picked up the pistol and stared at it for a long moment. Why hadn't the weapon fired?

One of the cardinal rules of any Special Forces team is mission preparation. That was especially true in Vietnam. I had checked out the weapon and the silencer myself. I had fired it six different times during rehearsals and again just prior to boarding the choppers for the target area. It had fired perfectly, each and every time. There had not been one misfire.

As I pondered this, Buck suddenly jumped into the ditch. His face reflected concern as he saw the blood covering the right side of my shirt and the path of blood that trailed down the side of my face. He glanced at the dead man, then back to me. The NVA had fallen back for the moment, but they would be back with a lot more friends very soon. Two of our men were wounded, and since our mission was now compromised, Buck wanted to call for the extraction helicopter. I quickly agreed.

We set up security and radioed for the choppers. Buck came over and began to patch me up as best he could. He noticed that I kept working the pistol back and forth, cocking the hammer and easing it down again. "What's wrong with the .38?" he asked.

I shook my head. "Nothing—that's the problem. There's nothing wrong with this weapon. I just don't understand it."

"Understand what?" he asked.

I related the story of the battle in the ditch and how, by all rights, I should be dead—but for some unexplainable reason the .38 had misfired, saving my life.

Buck, a weapons expert, took the pistol and ran it through the proper checks, then handed it back to me. He couldn't find anything wrong with it either. I was still staring at it while Buck secured a bandage, opened my shirt, and began to press it into the open gash in my shoulder.

"Well I'll be damned," he muttered.

"What's wrong?" I asked, trying to ignore the pain.

Buck ran his fingers down the length of the gold chain around my neck. They came to rest on the small crucifix.

"Brother, somebody was sure watching over your butt today."

"What is it, Buck? What are you talking about?" I asked.

Buck carefully removed the bloodstained chain from my neck and held the small cross in the palm of his big hand. Only then did I see it—in the exact center of the cross was a small indent. An indent caused by the hammer of the .38. It was this hammer that should have struck the firing pin and caused the weapon to fire.

During the struggle with the enemy, my cross had come out of my shirt and by some miracle dropped between the hammer of the pistol and the firing pin. When the NVA pulled the trigger, the hammer went forward but struck the center of the cross, blocking it from the firing pin and causing a misfire.

Was Buck right? Was I just lucky that day? At the time I thought so. But now I am convinced that I was fortunate enough to have experienced the wondrous works of God's guardian angels. My wife firmly believes that my life was spared that day in order that I might live to write this book. Could she be right?

## 23
# *The Angel of Ward 3-A*

*An angel stood and met my gaze,*
*Through the low doorway of my tent;*
*The tent is struck, the vision stays—*
*I only know she came and went.*

—JAMES RUSSELL LOWELL, ''She Came and Went''

AMONG THE 58,022 NAMES ETCHED INTO THE BLACK granite wall of the Vietnam Veterans Memorial in Washington, D.C., are those of eight military women: seven from the United States army and one from the United States air force. They were all members of the nursing profession, and as such paid the supreme sacrifice for their country in the Vietnam war.

Although thousands of their sisters were involved in that conflict, surprisingly little has been written about them. There is good news, however. Through the efforts of a number of former nurses of that era, a Nurses War Memorial statue will soon be placed a short distance from the black granite wall in honor of their service to the country. It is a monument that is well-deserved and long overdue.

For the countless wounded who passed through the hands of these brave women (myself included, on three separate occasions) I can only say thank you. Thank you for being there in my hours of pain and fear. Thank you for the kind words of reassurance, for the gentle touch of a caring hand, and for taking the time, no matter how busy you were, to come by and check on me. You were our angels in our time of need. God bless each and every one of you.

The following story demonstrates the strength of these women. It is the story of a woman whose determination and strong belief in God served her and the patients committed to her care.

Twenty-four-year-old Lieutenant Lisa Howell made one last check of the patients on her ward. Satisfied that all was well, she went back to her small office and continued to update her medical records for the doctors who would be coming for early morning rounds. It had been another long night. There were only two shifts a nurse could work at the 12th Evacuation Hospital in Cu Chi, seven A.M. to seven P.M. and seven P.M. to seven A.M., and this had been Lisa's first time on the night shift.

Finishing the last of the charts, she leaned back in her chair and stared down the length of the Quonset hut that served as Ward 3-A. It was nearly five A.M.—only two more hours to go.

As she watched one of her patients shift position in his sleep, she thought of where she was and how she had come to be in Vietnam. She had been in the country less than a month, and it still seemed strangely unreal to her. Only two months ago she had been celebrating her twenty-fourth birthday in her hometown of Parsons, Kansas. The entire family, knowing where she was going, had been there: aunts, uncles, grandparents, and close friends from high school days. They had all been wonderful to her. It had been like Christmas in August. Now here she was, applying the skills of a profession that she had thought about and loved since she was a little girl.

When other little girls thought of being models or Hollywood starlets, Lisa had thought only of one day becoming a nurse. Being there when people were in need of help and comforting them appealed to her. She was a very caring person and had a way of casting a radiance of good feeling over all those with whom she came into contact. In a word, she was a natural for the nursing profession.

While in nursing school, she, like so many Americans, watched the nightly news reports on the war in Vietnam. The pictures were often graphic and showed the pain and suffering that accompany man's favorite pastime—the game of war.

One night, while watching the medivac helicopters lift out the wounded and amazed at the seemingly chaotic, yet well-organized dedication of the medical staff who hurried the wounded from those birds of mercy and into the evac hospitals, she felt a sense of excitement and an immediate urge to help. That was where she should be. In Vietnam, where she could do the most good.

The following morning, she had gone to the local army recruiting office and had become a member of the military family. That was how Lieutenant Lisa Howell had come to be at the 12th Evac Hospital in Cu Chi, sitting in a Quonset hut, surrounded by the men of the United States army's Twenty-fifth Infantry Division.

The doctors soon arrived. She made the rounds with them and her relief before going to her room for some badly needed sleep. After removing her jungle boots, she leaned back against her bunk and took the Bible from the nightstand next to her bed. It was a Bible her mother had given her. Lisa was from a solid Christian home, and it was a rare occurrence for her not to read a passage from the Holy Book before going to bed. She read her favorite verses from the book of Psalms, then said a prayer for a young soldier who had died on her ward only minutes before she had gone on duty. As she always did, Lisa asked God to provide her with the strength to face each day's challenge and to protect her and those around her from harm. Soon, the young combat nurse was fast asleep.

Awake again by four in the afternoon, Lisa showered, dressed, and went to the mess hall for a bite to eat. The only conversation around the table that afternoon dealt with a rumor that intelligence had received word of a possible night attack against the base by North Vietnamese regulars.

The talk frightened Lisa, but the other nurses who had been in Vietnam for some time told her not to worry. They received these kinds of reports all the time, but an actual attack was a rarity. Oh, there might be a few mortar rounds fired into the camp, but that was about the extent of any attack they could expect from the NVA.

Lisa left the mess hall and returned to her room. An uneasy feeling hung over her like a gray cloud. She could not explain it, but somehow she sensed that something bad was going to happen. Despite the reassurance of her fellow nurses, it was a feeling that she could not shake. That night, as she started to leave her room for her shift, she paused a moment, then for some reason took the Bible from the nightstand. Clutching it tightly to her chest, she took the book with her to work that night. It was something she had never done before.

The nurses going off shift made good-natured remarks about her arriving with the Bible and again reassured her there was nothing to worry about. After all, they were totally surrounded by the combat-hardened men of the Twenty-fifth Infantry Division. No NVA unit could hope to battle their way through the entire twenty-fifth and reach the rows of hospital Quonset huts.

(Little did the American command or the American personnel at Cu Chi realize at the time, but they were sitting right on top of a central NVA tunnel complex that extended a distance of twenty-five miles in all directions. The NVA didn't have to come through the wire—they were already inside, sitting seventy-five to a hundred feet directly under the American compound and the hospital.)

Normally, another nurse would have been on duty with Lisa that night, but because there had been little fighting over the past few weeks, American casualties had been light. Ward 3-A contained only nine wounded men, less than a fourth of its total capacity. When asked if she would like another nurse on duty with her, Lisa had refused. All too often the wards were filled to overflowing with wounded and the nurses had to endure grueling workloads and countless hours without sleep. Now was a good time for many of them to get caught up. This light workload would not last forever, and they all knew it. She could handle it alone. Let the others get some rest.

The first few hours of her shift went by quickly. Lisa moved from bed to bed administering medications, talking and joking with her patients, and even writing a letter for a man who had lost one hand and had severe burns on the other. By doing these things she was able to shut out the feelings of impending disaster for a little while. However, by midnight, the ward was quiet, the patients all sleeping. The only sound was the hum of the heavy generators that powered the camp.

The first incoming rounds hit at exactly one A.M. They landed at the southern end of the camp, near the ammunition bunkers. The heavy roar of the explosions traveled like thunder between the Quonset huts, and the ground seem to shake. A second series soon followed, to the east this time.

The patients were wide-awake by now, fear and nervousness painfully clear in their young faces. Lisa quickly moved from bed to bed, pulling the mattress from the empty bed next to each patient and tossing it on the floor, then easing the wounded out of bed and onto the floor. She then jerked off the mattress they had vacated and placed it over them. One by one she worked her way along the line until all nine were under cover. Not until she had finished did she realize her hands were visibly shaking. She was terrified, yet she had functioned like a veteran.

Outside, the incoming rounds were coming so fast now that they were impossible to count. They seemed to be hitting everywhere at once. A sudden blast blew out two of the Plexiglas windows at the far end of Ward 3-A and tore a gaping hole in the wall next to the far door. Some of the patients were calling for her to get down, to find cover and stay put.

The sudden sound of small-arms fire rang out, mixed with the heavy thud of American mortars firing. Machine guns from the towers and the perimeter bunkers opened fire. The patients began throwing the mattresses off and screaming, "My God! It's a major attack! We've got to get out of here!"

Lisa ran to them. Pushing them back down and covering them again with a mattress, she told them they were safer where they were than outside running around. Everything would be all right, but they had to stay down. No sooner had she said that than a new sound was added to the chaos outside: the clear and distinct sound of Russian AK-47s, the NVA's favorite weapon of choice. This new gunfire was coming from inside the camp. The enemy had penetrated their defenses and were now moving from building to building, tossing in high-explosive satchel charges and grenades, then shooting those who ran outside.

Lisa rushed back to her small office. Two M-16 rifles stood in the corner and a .45 pistol lay on top of the file cabinet. The magazines for all three weapons were sitting next to the pistol. Lisa quickly looked at each of the weapons. What should she do? Which one should she take?

Before she could make her decision, two nurses burst through the door, half-carrying, half-dragging a wounded soldier. He was covered in blood, as were the nurses. Lisa quickly helped them get the man on a mattress on the floor, then grabbed some morphine and bandages. As they worked on the wounded soldier, the other nurses told of the nightmare going on outside.

There were wounded everywhere. NVA sappers and commandos were running wild in the camp, shooting at everything and everyone, while other NVA were blowing up any building they could reach before being shot down. The confusion was so widespread that some units of the 25th were firing at each other. Ward 7-B had taken a direct hit. While the medical personnel were trying to put out the fires and help the wounded, two NVA sappers, wearing nothing but loincloths and headbands, their bodies covered with black grease, had run through the ward firing their automatic weapons at everyone, killing a number of the wounded, one doctor, and two corpsmen, and wounding one of the nurses. It was a nightmare.

The sounds of weapons fire were right outside the door now. Lisa ran to the office again. Quickly she looked at the weapons. She grabbed a rifle and pushed one of the magazines into place and released the bolt. The rifle was now loaded and ready to perform its purpose: to kill.

As she started out of the office with the rifle under her arm, she hesitated for a moment. Her Bible was lying in the center of the desk. She looked at the rifle, then at the Bible. How ironic, she thought. One promises life—the other takes it away. Her whole body was trembling now. Could she shoot anyone? She didn't think so. Quickly grabbing the Bible, she ran out into the ward with a rifle in one hand and a Bible in the other.

Sergeant Paul Kirkland, one of the patients, had crawled over to the nurses to help in any way he could. Of the wounded on the ward, the sergeant was in the best shape. His wounds had almost healed, and he had only a few more days to go on the ward.

Lisa passed him the weapon. "It's loaded," she said, "hopefully we won't need it. But if we do, you don't fire until I tell you to, Sergeant. That's an order."

Sergeant Kirkland smiled as he nodded that he understood. Lisa was shocked at herself. That was the first official order she had ever given, and she had just given it to a combat-hardened vet who had seen more action than she ever would. Then again, maybe not. The night wasn't over yet.

A ringing sound echoed through the ward as a line of bullets tore holes along the right wall of the Quonset hut. Had the patients still been in their beds along that wall, every one of them would have been hit. Luckily they were on the floor and covered by the mattresses. "What are we going to do?" asked one of the nurses, trying hard to control the panic in her voice.

Lisa calmly opened her Bible and replied, "We are going to pray like we've never prayed before." Looking at those around her, she began, " 'The Lord is my shepherd, I shall not want . . .' "

The others quickly joined in. They had just finished the verse when, suddenly, two NVA grenades rolled through the door of Ward 3-A. "Grenades!" yelled the sergeant, pushing the women down and covering them with his body as best he could. But after a full minute, the grenades did not explode. "I don't believe it! They're all duds," said Sergeant Kirkland.

Lisa continued to pray. The door swung open wide and two NVA soldiers stood boldly at the end of the hall, weapons at the ready to quickly dispatch anyone they saw in the building. "Oh, God . . . please. Let your angels blind them to our presence," whispered Lisa quietly under breath.

The NVA came halfway down the center of the hut, their eyes alert, searching left, then right. They apparently didn't see anyone. Sergeant Kirkland couldn't believe it. They were almost directly in front of him. Slowly, he started to raise his M-16.

Lisa gently touched his hand and pushed the weapon back down. As the sergeant looked at her, she shook her head slowly from side to side. Her hand was resting firmly on the Bible, her eyes closed, and she was praying. The nurses beside her clutched each other's hands, their eyes closed as well, waiting for whatever was going to happen next.

Having reached the center of the hut, the two enemy soldiers looked at each other, then shrugged their shoulders. They obviously didn't see anyone in the building. Turning, they quickly ran back out the door and into the night. Sergeant Kirkland let out a deep breath and, placing his hand over Lisa's, which was still holding firm to the Bible, said, ''That's a very powerful weapon you have there, Lieutenant.''

The following morning Lieutenant Lisa Howell, Sergeant Kirkland, and the two nurses who had been with her that night were ordered to report to the operations center. Word of what had happened on Ward 3-A had spread like wildfire through the camp, and the commander wanted to hear the story himself. After they had finished their reports they were the subject of what some would call an inquisition. Intelligence officers suggested that it was not a miracle that had saved them, but rather the fact that the NVA often doped up their sappers before an attack to send them into a wild frenzy. Obviously, the two NVA who had entered Ward 3-A were high on drugs and that was why they had not seen anyone in the building.

That would be the command's official explanation for what had happened on Ward 3-A that nightmare night in 1968. But those who were there and witnessed it knew the truth. Lieutenant Lisa Howell had had a choice between two weapons that night, and she had chosen the more powerful of the two: the word of God and the protection of the angels.

# THE
# DESERT WAR

DURING THE IRAQI WAR MANY BEHIND-THE-SCENES ACtivities escaped the media coverage of Operation Desert Shield. It was not by chance, but rather by design. And for a very good reason. The soldiers carrying out these clandestine operations were members of America's most elite units. While newscasters speculated about what Saddam Hussein was doing, these troops were deep inside Iraqi territory collecting vital information and intelligence on enemy positions, troop movements, and enemy command posts.

It was factual information, not speculation. Its value to the Coalition forces cannot be measured. Following the war, the commander of the Coalition, General Norman Schwarzkopf, heralded the outstanding job performed by these silent warriors of the night, praising both their skill and their daring throughout the Iraqi campaign.

Although I retired from the U.S. army in 1988, I had been a member of Special Forces for over twenty years and knew many of those involved in the Iraqi war. When I decided to write this book, I contacted a few of my friends at Fort Bragg, North Carolina, and inquired if they knew of anyone who might have experienced something along the lines of the stories in this book. To my surprise, they had. Actually it shouldn't have been that much of a surprise considering that so many of the Bible's stories take place in the very places the Iraqi war was fought.

One friend told me that there had been something, but he wasn't sure those involved would want to see it in print. He would call me back. The following day, I received a call from two old friends who had been with the team that had observed a spiritual happening in the desert of Iraq. They agreed to relate the details to me.

The story was told to me by members of a recon team who had been involved in the war only days after the invasion of Kuwait. I served with both of these men at one time or another and know them to be highly capable, intelligent, and as tough as they come. Their character is above reproach. I am grateful to them for allowing me to share this experience with you.

I will advise the reader, however, that for security reasons I have altered the team designation and the names of those involved, due to the nature of the job facing these brave and heroic men. This in no way alters the facts of what occurred one dark night in the desert sands of Iraq.

# 24
# *An Angelic Guide*

*Behold, I send an Angel before thee, to keep thee in thy way . . .*

—Exodus 23:20

WITHIN DAYS OF THE INVASION OF KUWAIT, A NUMBER of American Special Operations detachments from Fort Bragg, North Carolina, arrived in Saudi Arabia. One of those teams was Detachment A-505 under the command of Captain Martin Long and his executive officer, Chief Warrant Officer Thomas Shell. The two units formed the nucleus of a highly trained twelve-man combat team whose résumé included missions in Panama, El Salvador, and Colombia. In Colombia, the team had advised and conducted operations with the military arm of the Colombian Drug Enforcement Agency. Highly proficient and equally tough, A-505 could handle anything Saddam Hussein had in mind for the allies.

The team sergeant of A-505 is Master Sergeant

Robert Howard, a veteran of Vietnam and a former member of American's elite antiterrorist unit known as the Delta Force.

Following a week of intense briefings and intelligence analysis of satellite photos, the mission launch order finally arrived from Washington to begin intelligence operations against the Iraqi forces of Saddam Hussein.

The detachment's mission required the twelve-man team to be broken down into four three-man units. These small units would be deployed at the four sections of a preplotted quadrangle, with each three-man team responsible for conducting reconnaissance in their sector and reporting back to the Coalition command in Saudi Arabia.

Each unit would be responsible for reporting the exact locations of tanks, troop movement and fixed locations, and locations of antiaircraft weapons, command posts, land mines, trenches, bunkers, and barbed-wire obstructions. It was a monumental task, considering that all this had to be accomplished in the very heart of enemy territory. But it is specifically for this type of situation that Special Operations teams are trained.

Each unit would work independent of the others. They were advised that should they run into trouble, they were totally on their own. Due to the distance inside enemy territory in which they would operating, any rescue attempt to save them would be marginal at best—if forthcoming at all. This was clearly understood by all members of the detachment. This may sound harsh to many readers, but the invasion of Kuwait caught the world by surprise, and the formulation of any type of military response would take time to organize. At the outset, Allied support was very limited, but building each day. These intelligence missions, however, could not wait. General Schwarzkopf and the Coalition forces had to know what they were up against.

After midnight on August 23, 1990, the detachment departed a Saudi airfield aboard a C-130 cargo plane. At an altitude of fifteen thousand feet, the first three-man unit exited the aircraft using the HALO method (high altitude low opening) better known as skydiving to the civilian. The plane then made its way to the remaining three corners of the quadrangle, with each unit exiting on both voice and light commands of the pilot.

The team operating in the northeast corner of the quadrangle consisted of Master Sergeant Robert Howard, Staff Sergeant Jack Dyer, and Staff Sergeant Richard Cates. Once on the ground, the team buried their chutes and activated a satellite transponder, a device that uses satellite computers to lock on to the transponder signal and can give the operator a fix on his exact location to within twenty-five feet. Finding where they were on the map, the team moved off to the South. Locating a long twisting gully just before daylight, they placed camouflage netting over themselves and holed up for the day. The Iraqis had no idea that they had been invaded by the Special Operations command.

Waiting until just before midnight, when guards were likely to be somewhat inattentive or asleep, the team moved out from their gully hideaway and began to prowl their target area. That first night they encountered a wealth of information on fixed troop positions and bunker complexes, and even located four mobile Scud missiles on platforms. The Coalition command was ecstatic over the amount of valuable intelligence coming from the teams out of the quadrangle.

By the end of the week, a complete and detailed map showing enemy fortifications, weapons, and troop size had begun to be formulated, not only in that one quadrangle, but across the entire Iraqi line as other teams were inserted into Iraq and Kuwait. Few Americans realized that the Coalition briefings carried by all the major networks and CNN around the clock contained information that had been provided to the command by these brave warriors of the night. One can only imagine how Saddam must have felt seeing the exact coordinates of his ''secret'' units and locations being broadcast around the world on the ''Today'' show, CNN, and ''Good Morning America.''

However, there is always a price to be paid for success. Although no exact numbers can or will be given in the near future, these operations did not come about without the loss of life. At one time up to ten A-detachments were working behind-the-line recon missions. We shall only say that incidental contact led to firefights with Iraqi troops in which American casualties were sustained.

On the night of September 12, 1990, Master Sergeant Howard and his team were preparing to go out on another recon when they detected enemy movement on their right and left flanks. The Iraqis were searching for the source of the information coming out of their area and were certain that American commandos were behind the reports Saddam was seeing every morning on his television. They had to be found and either captured or eliminated.

Staff Sergeant Cates reported an Iraqi motorized unit was now moving up with searchlights and ground troops. Beams of light coming from the sky could be seen in the distance. Iraqi helicopters had joined in the search and were sweeping the desert floor with their powerful searchlights as well. Fortunately for Howard's team, they had been conducting their recon in a northerly direction and less than two miles from the Saudi border. If they could get close enough to that border for the Coalition forces to provide artillery and air support, they might have a chance. Speed was of the utmost importance now.

In a game of moves and countermoves, Howard's team and the Iraqis played a deadly game of hide-and-seek. The Americans realized that all they had going for them was the darkness. If they could not reach Saudi lines by daylight, the advantage shifted to the Iraqis. Their helicopters could easily cut off any escape across the border and capture or kill the fleeing team. Everyone was aware of that—especially Howard, Cates, and Dyer.

It was a frantic race against the clock, a race that was made even more difficult by having to double-back or swing wide away from the direction of the border to avoid enemy patrols that vastly outnumbered the three Americans. But these were men who seldom if ever panicked. They accepted these setbacks in stride and continued making their way across the desert sands. One hour before daylight, they dropped to the ground and checked their coordinates. If Howard was right, and he was certain he was, they were less than one mile from safety. Behind them, the searchlights and Iraqi army continued to search. "We're almost there," whispered Howard to his two companions. "Only a mile to go."

It was at that moment, when Howard started to rise, that he noticed a small black object in the sand highlighted by the dim starlight. He had an idea what it was, but to be sure, he reached out his hand and slowly began to brush the sand away from around the black circular object. "Oh, Jeez," uttered Cates under his breath. "Mine," whispered Dyer. Cates nodded.

They had stumbled into an Iraqi minefield. How far in, they had no idea. Howard looked behind them. The Iraqi search party was heading straight for them. There was no time to back out of the field, and no telling what lay ahead of them. Getting on the radio, Howard made contact with headquarters and gave his location. He then informed them of his situation and requested artillery support to slow the search party coming up behind them. Headquarters approved the action and told him that a Saudi company of infantry were moving to the border to assist them if they could make it the last mile. Wishing them good luck, headquarters ended the conversation. It was now all up to the team.

Pulling their trench knives, the three began to probe the sand in front of them as the crawled slowly forward. They found two more mines. If there was one thing the Iraqis believed in, it was mines—lots of them. Within minutes the sound of artillery shells whistled high over their heads and began to explode in and around the Iraqi search party. This would hold them at bay for a little while, but not for long.

The probing was a tedious affair, but even worse, it was time-consuming. Howard estimated that they had less than one hour before sunrise. In the daylight the Iraqi choppers were sure to spot them, and they'd be like sitting ducks in the minefield.

Wiping the sweat from his eyes, Cates looked at the horizon. The first gray lines of approaching dawn had appeared.

"We're running out of time, Sarge," said Cates.

"I know," answered Howard. After twenty minutes of probing they had managed to advance less than one hundred yards and had uncovered thirteen mines. "If you boys are owed any favors from the man upstairs, now'd be a good time to call 'em in."

Dyer, a devout Christian and the new father of a daughter born only three days before he had left for Saudi Arabia, stuck his knife in the sand and clasped his hands firmly together. "That's not a bad idea, Top. After all, who knows? Jesus himself may have walked over this very spot at one time."

Howard and Cates stopped their work and stared at the young father for a moment, then Howard reached out and all three joined hands and recited the Lord's Prayer. When they had finished, they experienced a feeling of great calm pass over them.

"Well, at least, if we don't get out of this, God will know we were thinking of Him at the end," said Howard.

The three returned to their work. After a few minutes, Cates shouted, "Look!" and pointed to the sand in front of them.

A glowing, almost mistlike cloud had appeared, hovering twenty yards in front of them and a few feet above the ground.

"What is that?" asked Dyer.

Neither Howard nor Cates answered. They were as amazed by the sight as Dyer.

The cloud came forward a few feet, then moved back, weaving to the right, then left, then back right again.

"What's it doing?" asked Howard of no one in particular.

"If I didn't know any better, I'd say it was trying to show us a way through this minefield," replied Cates.

The three watched the glowing cloud for a few minutes. Again it repeated the maneuvers, this time coming closer, then weaving its way through the minefield. "What d'you think, Top?" asked Dyer, "Do we follow it?"

Howard looked at the horizon. Daylight was only minutes away. The artillery had stopped firing and the Iraqi search unit was moving toward them again and they were still more than a half-mile from the Saudi border. Their options were limited. Stay there and be captured and led off to an Iraqi prison. Be shot to pieces in a minefield by Iraqi helicopter gunships. Make a mad dash for it and be blown to pieces by a mine. Or believe in their hearts that this strange glowing light that had appeared before them was God-sent and put their fate in its hands. Only one option offered any hope.

"Let's go," said Howard, rising to his feet. "We're all going to see God someday. Might as well see if it'll be today."

The three men began to trot toward the light, following its exact path as it wove its way toward the Saudi border.

When they were less than fifty yards from safety, the sun rose and the light vanished. A company of Saudi troops waved and cheered them on the last leg of their trip. The Saudi officer in charge came up to Howard. "We knew there were mines between us. One of my men found one as we started to come to your aid, but we had no idea where the mines were. What you and your men did was one of the bravest things we have ever seen."

Breathing hard, Howard asked, "Did you see it?"

"See what?" answered the Saudi officer.

"A glowing light. It was in front of us as we ran."

Looking at Howard strangely, he replied, "No, Sergeant. My men and I have been here for over an hour, and we saw no light. We were not even sure where you were until you stood up."

# ANGELS
# EVERYWHERE

# 25

# Guardian Angels Know No Boundaries

*Although they do not go about with weapons and combat gear, the missionary is certainly a soldier; his only weapons a Bible and a strong faith in his commander, God.*

JOHN G. PATON AND HIS WIFE WERE MISSIONARIES WHO had accepted a posting in the New Hebrides. Previous attempts by various groups to bring the word of God to the natives of these islands had met with hostile resistance by the local witch doctors and shamans who saw this new religion as a threat to their own power over the people. Eventually, through threats and intimidation, they had managed to drive each missionary group out of the islands.

Knowing of the island's past history, the Patons refused to accept the fact that God's word could reach all but those of the New Hebrides. Determined to succeed where others had failed, they arrived at their post and immediately began to clean up the area and make repairs on their new home and the small church that had been built by earlier missionaries.

When those tasks were completed, they sent out word to the people of all the islands that they had arrived and welcomed anyone who wished to attend their church services. The first few weeks, no one dared to visit the Patons for fear of bringing the wrath of the witch doctors down on them. Still determined, the Patons decided that if the people would not come to then, they would go to the people.

Traveling from village to village, they found that many of the chiefs were surprised to see them. The other missionaries had always remained at their small church and were fearful of venturing far from the protection of their home. The new teachers were different. They did not hide and hope for the natives to come to them; they trusted enough in their God to come to the villages of the people and walk freely among them without fear. This impressed many of the chiefs, and they soon agreed to allow those of their people who wished to learn more about the missionaries and their God to attend services at the mission.

For a while all went well, but before long the Patons began to hear talk among some of their converts about a powerful chief who had a village on the far side of the island. This chief's witch doctor was spreading evil words about the missionaries and warning his chief that the Patons were actually there to take away his power and enslave his people.

Upon hearing of this, John Paton made plans to visit this chief at his village to show that the shaman's words were false and to invite the powerful chieftain to the mission. The converts, hearing of this plan, quickly rushed to the mission and after many hours of talking, convinced the missionary to delay his visit.

The chief, hearing of the planned trip, asked his shaman what this meant. Seeing an opportunity to rid himself of the troublesome missionaries, the witch doctor made a few incantations, shook a few rattles, then proclaimed that the visit was not meant to be one of peace, but rather a visit to test the power of the chief. Should that power prove weak, the missionaries would put a curse on the chief and steal away with all his people.

The chief went into a rage. Gathering all his warriors, he set out for the mission, intent on destroying the Patons and burning down all the buildings that surrounded them. The missionaries had to die.

The other natives, having heard of the approach of the powerful chief and his army, fled in a panic, leaving John Paton and his wife to face the oncoming tide of hatred alone. It was not a long wait.

As the sun began to set, the Patons heard the natives approaching through the jungle. They quickly entered their small home. Alone and totally defenseless, they had only prayer with which to fight their enemy. Outside, the natives surrounded the small mission and set fire to their torches. They would fire everything, then, when the missionaries ran out, they would kill them.

The Patons repeated prayer after prayer, expecting to see flames licking at the door at any moment. All during the terror-filled night they prayed for Almighty God to deliver them. Minutes soon turned into hours, and still the dreaded attack that they knew was imminent never came. When the sun rose again, the Patons were amazed to find that the natives had left. Smoke drifted up from the smoldering torches that had been lit, but never used. They lay scattered all around the mission in a near-perfect circle. What had happened to the natives? Why had they not attacked the helpless couple?

Having survived the night and escaped certain death, thanks to a merciful God, the missionaries thought it best to leave and live to return another day.

And return they did. A little over a year later John Paton happened to encounter the very same chieftain who had come that night to kill him and his wife. The old chief had since been converted to Christianity and apologized to the missionary for both his people and his actions that night. They had been led down the devil path by the shaman, but all of that was over. Now they were Christians and had found new life in Jesus Christ.

Unable to let the moment pass without asking the question that had bothered him and his wife since that terrible night, John took the chief aside and asked, "I know you have accepted Christ, but I must ask you. That night you could have easily set fire to our mission and killed me and my wife. Why didn't you?"

The chief stared at him in surprise for a moment, then explained, "If you had not had so many guards around the house, we would have surely done as you say that night."

Now it was the Reverend Paton's turn to show surprise.

"But chief, there were no men there—just my wife and me."

The chief shook his head from side to side as he replied, "No, my brother, you are wrong. There were many men, perhaps as many as a hundred. They were big men in shining garments and they held drawn swords in their hands as they circled the mission station. My warriors became frightened and were afraid to attack, so we thought it best to leave. So we did.''

Only then did John Paton realize that God's angels had been with them throughout the long ordeal. The chief agreed that there could be no other explanation for what he and his warriors saw that night.

## 26

# Angels and the Cosmonauts of the USSR

FOR THOSE WHO HAVE A STRONG RELIGIOUS BELIEF IT is easy to accept the many wonders that occur throughout the world and credit those happenings to God or His angels. But what of those who flatly deny the existence of God, let alone angels? What if that disbelief is not the mindset of a single individual, but rather the official policy of an entire country? Not just any country, but a world superpower?

When Soviet cosmonauts first returned from orbiting the earth on April 12, 1961, Yuri A. Gagarin, a Soviet air force officer, quickly proclaimed that they had not encountered any God. Nor had they seen the often-referred-to place known as heaven on this historic first flight in space. The Soviet Union was quick to point out that Gagarin's statement gave credence to the atheistic philosophy of the Soviet

Union and therefore should do away with such myths as the existence of a supreme being and a place called heaven with streets of gold.

Needless to say, the Soviets relished the opportunity to discredit all religion worldwide and went to great pains to keep the story of Gagarin's trip and the nonexistence of heaven or God front-page news for many months after that.

For nearly twenty-five years, whenever the matter of religion came up, the Soviets would smile and quickly cite the results of their first manned space flight, which had unequivocally "proven" that all religion was based solely on fiction. There was no heaven—there was no God . . .

The atheistic hard-core Communist line that had existed since 1918 and had been reinforced in 1961 was about to be dealt a stunning blow that would send a shock wave throughout Russia and the rest of the religious world.

By the summer of 1985 the Soviet space program had advanced at an amazing rate. They had managed to establish a permanent station in space. Here the cosmonauts could stay for extended periods of time and conduct their experiments on a daily basis. They named the space station Salyut 7. Orbiting miles above the earth, a team of three cosmonauts were into the 155th day of their mission, and until that point all had gone well.

Commander Atkov, the mission control officer, and two cosmonauts, Captain Soloviev and Captain Kizim, had just began their daily routine checks at the control panel when suddenly a dazzling orange light enveloped their space station. The light was so blinding that at first the Soviets feared that there had been an explosion or that a sudden fire had erupted somewhere within the station. The light had been so bright that for the first few minutes all three men were totally blinded.

When their vision slowly began to return, they moved to the portholes of the space station and looked out. What they saw startled them. In shock, Commander Atkov quickly radioed Soviet ground control. From the sound of the commander's voice, ground control knew that something was wrong aboard the Salyut 7.

Hurriedly, Atkov told them of the sudden burst of light that had seemed like an explosion. Were there injuries? asked ground control. Was there a fire? What had caused it? Ground control was in a near panic themselves by this time and continued to ask questions in rapid-fire succession.

Atkov quickly assured them that everyone was all right and that the space station had not sustained any damage. All systems were responding properly and there had been no explosion or fire. There was, however, something outside the windows of the space station.

"What is it?" demanded ground control. "What do you see?"

"We are seeing faces," said Atkov in a nervous voice.

Ground control immediately ordered that the commander repeat his message again—this time very slowly.

Atkov did as instructed. Slowly and distinctly, Commander Atkov described what they were looking at from the portals of the space station.

"Outside our space station, we are observing . . . or I should say, being observed . . . by seven giant figures. They were in human form and appear to be several hundred feet tall. They have wings that span the width of a jetliner, and above each of their heads there are radiant halos of gold. They appear to be what we call on earth ... angels. Their faces are bright and they are watching us even now as I speak.''

Needless to say, Soviet ground control was at a momentary loss for words. If the man was to be believed, it meant that the figures Commander Atkov described were easily keeping pace with the Salyut 7 that was orbiting the earth at nearly five miles a second.

The seven apparitions were observed for a full ten minutes, then, as suddenly as they had appeared, they abruptly vanished.

In a hurried and excited exchange between the space station and ground control, the cosmonauts again described, in detail, everything they had observed. Commander Atkov realized how strange all this must sound to those on the ground. There was little doubt in his mind that the Kremlin had already been notified of this rather bizarre and highly unusual report. The three aboard the space station were certain that ground control did not believe them and felt that all three were possibly teetering on the brink of insanity. Therefore, after several days had passed, and they had time to discuss it among themselves, they notified control that they were convinced that the angel sighting had occurred because of some inexplicable reason that had caused some sort of group hallucination.

Soviet officials at ground control expressed relief that the three had regained their senses and had logically come to this conclusion. The mission was now back on schedule and all was going well.

Twelve days later, on the 167th day of the mission, the Soviets launched the Soyuz T-12. On board were Commander Volk and two officers, Major Dzhanibovek and Captain Savistkaya. Their mission was to link up with the Salyut 7 to conduct further experiments. The docking of the two spacecraft went without incident. Now there were six cosmonauts aboard the space station.

The new arrivals were on board less than one hour when the space station was once again enveloped in a dazzling orange light that temporarily blinded all aboard. Ground control was immediately alerted. They were stunned by the renewed report. What did they see this time? asked ground control.

"We can see the faces of seven angels ... smiling," replied Commander Atkov. "They are smiling as if they are sharing some glorious secret with us. They are exactly the same size as before. There is a radiance about them. I cannot explain it, and we all see them."

There was a long moment of silence at ground control. Then Atkov came on the radio again. "They are gone! They stayed only a few minutes and now ... they are gone. We cannot see them anymore."

These exchanges between the space station and ground control were maintained in the strictest secrecy in the Soviet Union and were never known to the outside world until a top Soviet engineer who had been a member of the space program left Russia and came to the United States.

Any and all references to the incident were forbidden and all questions referring to the subject received no response from the officials of the Soviet Union.

Did the crew of the space station Salyut 7 actually gaze upon the faces of seven angels? Perhaps Atkov and his crew were overly tired. After all, they had been aboard the station for over one hundred and fifty days. That is a long time to be confined to a small area, and the stress factor can only be imagined. But then how does one explain the second sighting witnessed by a crew that had been aboard only one hour?

According to Colonel Yengeny Petrov, former commander of the Soviet cosmonauts, the members of their space program are selected "for their mental and physical excellence, as well as their spiritual and ethical qualities, ideological views, and social attitudes."

That the Communists were strict atheists and that the members of the space program met all the above standards required by these same Communists make this case even more intriguing.

Were seven sworn atheists granted the privilege of witnessing what millions of Christians often pray for? Did they look upon the faces of angels? You be the judge.

# *Amazing and Inspiring True Stories of Divine Intervention*

## *They are with us always...*

**ANGELS**                                      72331-X/$4.99 US
   by Hope Price

**ANGELS AMONG US**   77377-5/$4.99 US/$5.99 Can
   by Don Fearheiley

### *They happen when you least expect them and need them most...*

**MIRACLES**                              77652-9/$4.99 US/$5.99 Can
   by Don Fearheiley